UNFINISHED BUSINESS

J.L. FREDRICK

Lovstad Publishing
Poynette, Wisconsin
Lovstadpublishing@live.com

UNFINISHED BUSINESS

First Edition

ISBN: 0615813089
ISBN-13: 978-0615813080

Printed in the United States of America

Cover design by Lovstad Publishing

For Michael W.
He is gone but not forgotten.

More Novels by J.L. Fredrick

Across the Dead Line
Across the Second Dead Line
The Private Journal of Clancy Crane
The Other End of the Tunnel
Another Shade of Gray
The Gaslight Knights
Thunder in the Night
The Great Train Robbery of Monroe County
Mad City Bust
September Ten
Aftermath
Cursed by the Wind

Non-Fiction
Rivers, Roads, and Rails

Unfinished Business

As ghost towns go, most of them are double-dipped in the history pot and sprinkled with embellishments—facts or fallacies, makes no difference. If it sounds reasonable, most people will accept the stories. Nearly every mining town that faded into the dusty, lost caverns of times gone by, though, does possess some colorful background, if only by virtue of the colorful individuals who staked prospecting claims and populated the sprouting settlement that eventually became a town. These towns were usually lawless. Add a few saloons, brothels and gambling parlors; throw in a bunch of fortune-crazed prospectors with a little gold dust in their leather pouches; stir in a generous portion of entrepreneurs who knew how to get that gold dust into their possession. Now you have the high octane mixture that propelled these towns into the glorious, wild tales that add the zesty flavor to our past. Silver Spring had been one of those towns.

But unfortunately, its demise came some twenty years later amidst a growing dark reputation. The mines played out and the population diminished faster than it had grown. Then the manhunt for a ruthless killer resulted in fire that destroyed the entire town, except for the only brick building—Tanglewood Lodge.

As if the mining rush had been some sort of natural disturbance that swept through the forest and then receded, the woods grew back like a jungle over collapsing mine shafts; prairie grass camouflaged the ruined city and hid the abandoned railroad beds. Nature reclaimed the land and healed the wounds that man had inflicted upon it.

And then... along came the "boys" in the Twenty-first Century. Robby Gladstone, Grant Kraemer, and Keith Bradley, new graduates of Wellington High with sights set on their first college term had earned a summer—their *last* summer as kids—to just have fun, to do whatever they wanted to do. A few restrictions applied, and a few responsibilities still kept them close to home, just as their well-to-do parents intended—after all, college would take them away for the next four years, at least, and maybe more.

With a couple of old journals that Robby found in a box of his late grandfather's belongings tucked away in the attic, the boys discovered the clues that could lead them to an unimaginable treasure. And as far as they could tell, no one else alive was aware of the treasure's existence. Trouble was... the treasure—an undisclosed number of seventy-pound ingots of pure silver and gold—were hidden in taboo territory, Silver Spring. But the journals also provided more information disproving a legend that claimed the presence of an evil spirit in the old ghost town. It had been a contrived plan to keep everyone away. But now the contrivers were all dead, and the treasure had never been recovered. Secrecy would be the key to the boys' success.

So their undaunted young spirits led them to the place on a treasure hunt; their ingenuity designed their methods; the results altered the course of their lives forever.

And so the saga continues. Time is the present. The town has been resurrected in replica fashion, and the "boys" are knee-deep in adventure they couldn't possibly have imagined.

1

In the early morning light Keith Bradley leaned on the railing surrounding the deck outside his front window, the very window from where he had caught his first glimpse of Silver Spring as it really was—a ruined city of the Nineteenth Century consisting of no more than a grid work of stone foundations, the skeletons of buildings that could only be imagined then. Nothing else was left except the old hotel—Tanglewood Lodge—miraculously, mysteriously still intact after all those years. Oh, how he had fallen in love with this place. Its charming beauty, its haunting serenity, and its enchanted past had captivated his interest that summer when he and his two best friends had experienced Silver Spring for the first time. And now, eight years later, the place still held his intrigue like the night sky holds the full moon.

A light haze unmolested yet by the rising sun drifted on the plateau stretching out before him. In the valley beyond, a vague fog blanketed the meadow and concealed Silver Creek that threaded its mysterious way among the hills. It was that same kind of fog he had awakened to on the morning of his first visit here, only then he had been down there in the valley *in* the fog, unaware of the fascinating future this hilltop held in store for him.

Now, eight years later, he had good reason to be proud of the development he and his two best friends had accomplished: Tanglewood Lodge, the only remaining sound structure of the lost city—the only building surviving the disastrous 1899 fire that destroyed the rest of the town, had been brought back to life with extensive refurbishing and modernization, thanks to the talented skills Keith obtained during his four and a half years studying civil engineering and architecture at the University of Colorado. Grand offices downstairs and three luxury apartments upstairs. The old hotel, had it been restored to its original state, could have been the focal point for tourists seeking an authentic ghost town edifice of the past—and its exterior did just that—however, it was also at the heart of their passion for this entire project, and it was only fitting that the "boys" should be permitted to enjoy the internal pleasures of this fabulous find without a daily parade of gawking sightseers. It was bad enough that the necessary clients sometimes populated their offices for hours, but the rules of limitation clearly stated that anything beyond the first step of the stairways required special invitation—they deserved their privacy.

He could see a few cars had accumulated in the parking area beside the Crystal Palace, and a couple more were just arriving; the cast members of the theatrical club were getting an early start on their Saturday morning rehearsal. The inaugural performance of *A Midsummer Night's Dream* would be performed on the Crystal Palace Stage, and it would be the debut for some of the newer members of the group. Virgil Thurston, the director, insisted on these early Saturday morning sessions to ensure the cast was well-prepared for opening night. Saturday was a busy day for some of the cast members portraying the 'ghosts' of Silver Spring for the tourists and casual visitors to the resurrected town during the business hours of the day. So Thurston demanded that the play rehearsals should be conducted *before* everyone was tired.

Keith sipped his morning coffee. He loved this time of day. As the fresh dawn air filled his lungs, he thought about how much he had enjoyed the presence of the volunteer theater group members roaming the streets in random pattern, clad in the attire of Nineteenth Century frontier, greeting Silver Spring visitors and performing their little skits on the streets and boardwalks. Certainly not *the main attraction*, but it was gaining popularity among the tourist crowd. Saturday was usually the day they staged a bank hold-up.

Munchkin jumped silently up on the railing and padded next to Keith, rubbing against his arm, looking for some early morning attention. Of the three cats that were rescued from the animal shelter in Wellington, Munchkin, a gray tabby with the IQ of Einstein, it seemed, had attached his affection to Keith almost immediately, and although all three felines spent much time together, when it came bedtime, Munchkin always found his way to Keith's apartment bedroom. He was the Sherlock Holmes of the three, always observant, always curious, always ready to seek out any intruding rodents that didn't belong within the confines of Tanglewood.

"Well, good morning, Munchkin," Keith said to the purring feline. He stroked the silky fur on Munchkin's head.

The cat looked up into Keith's eyes, blinked, and stretched his neck toward Keith's face, as if inviting a good morning kiss. "Mrrraow," came out amidst the purring.

Keith lowered his head so their noses touched. He had become quite fond of Munchkin, and the cat seemed to understand that and always showed his appreciation for the friendship.

"Looks like the actors are already here for practice this morning."

"Mrrraow." The cat stared a few moments toward the theater.

"Gonna be a beautiful day, looks like."

"Mrrraow."

"I suppose you'd like some breakfast, eh Munchkin?"

"Mrrrrrrrrrrrraowwwww."

"I'll take that as a yes. Let's find something to eat."

2.

All the usual construction noise from the new Silver Spring Hotel had long ago moved inside where it wasn't `quite so abrasive to the rest of the world. On a Saturday there might not be too much going on, but to Keith's surprise, the carpet layers were there in full force, and furniture delivery trucks were already backing up to the door. Not that Keith would have minded the noise so much; it meant that the sixty-room hotel was that much closer to completion. The target opening date was only a couple of weeks away, and that meant increased traffic and activity in Silver Spring. It would be a welcomed addition to the fledgling town.

The hotel had taken the longest to build, because it had to meet more stringent building codes in accordance with laws regulating public accommodations. Although the hotel was to be as modern and elegant on the inside as any one might find in the present day, the 'Old Wild West' motif appeared on the outside, just as all the other buildings in the reconstructed town. The boys had made the requirement of anyone purchasing a lot and putting up a structure for a business—*it had to look like old Silver Spring.* They had already constructed several buildings on Main Street, some of them on the original stone foundations where possible. Keith had drawn up the construction plans while he was still in college, and for the design of the outer facades, he consulted Clancy Crane's journal for some modest descriptive details—the same journal that had led them to the hidden treasure. He handed over these blueprints to trusted contractors, and within a year, Silver Spring started to take shape in replicated fashion. Those buildings, bearing the names of some of the original stores in downtown *old* Silver Spring, now housed gift shops and boutiques, offering all sorts of gifts, souvenirs, novelties, books, clothing, and just opened, a bakery and candy store—all the things tourists crave. Those buildings became the construction guidelines for the rest of the town. At first, the boys feared that it would put too much restriction on potential business prospects, but in time there were businessmen and developers lined up to acquire the prime spots, and all agreed to the 'old' outward appearance.

Curious about how the interior of the new hotel was shaping up, Keith thought he should get dressed and walk over to the site just to snoop. But this wasn't his project, and he decided to wait for an invitation by the proprietor.

Keith's pride and joy of all his re-creations, though, was the Crystal Palace—the opera house theater, bearing the same name its predecessor was given in 1895. Because of its size and intended function, a slight deviation from the original layout of the town was required: built with its front entrance on Main Street, just as the original opera house had been, the new theater extended nearly the entire depth of the block and occupied the space of several adjacent original buildings as well. The Crystal Palace was intended to be the main attraction of the revived town, providing a venue for various types of entertainment. So far, it had operated only one summer and fall season, and its four hundred seats had been filled to near capacity for most of the shows, standing room only for some. By the time the show schedule began, the new Silver Spring had already attracted a great deal of attention from the locals, curiosity seekers mostly, as a result of numerous front page newspaper articles declaring that Mack, the resident evil ghost's siege was finally over, and that the ghost town, laying dormant for over a century, was being revitalized by three young sons of Wellington, the new owners of the territory that had been feared and avoided for so long.

The Bradley, Gladstone & Kraemer Real Estate Agency had quietly sprouted during their college years, and just as quietly acquired seven hundred acres of state-owned land—the land where Silver Spring had lived and died—the land that had been considered for so many years as useless and unwanted. Some people may have looked upon their ambitions as a waste of time and money, that local belief in a legend would have their project stymied from its very inception. But clever use of news media publicity changed all that, and now the would-be cynics were clamoring for a piece of the action, or the opportunity to enjoy the entertainment in that remote, rustic setting. Silver Spring was once again alive, and what it had to offer was in growing demand.

3

"The *McDonald's* franchise people are at it again." Robin Gladstone conveyed the news to his partners as he sat on one of the half-dozen wooden bar stools lined up in front of the mahogany bar. The front reception room of Tanglewood was the only part of the historic building, other than the exterior, that had retained a Nineteenth Century décor. Diminished in size from the original barroom and foremost entertainment hall, it had been restored to its original likeness, replete with an upright player-piano, pot-belly stove, and authentic antique furnishings. The only refreshment served across the original Tanglewood bar now, however, was coffee. Although it was functional as their favorite early morning meeting room, the replica 1890s saloon was intended more as an historic ornamental display for visitors.

"They still trying to get the lot next to the hotel?" Grant Kraemer asked. He sipped his coffee.

"Don't they understand?" Keith added. "The golden arches just won't fit in here."

"I've told 'em that, but they're being quite persistent. Now they want the lot next to the Crystal Palace." Robin

Gladstone generally conducted the delicate business of real estate sales; his seven years of schooling as a lawyer had also instilled in him the art of diplomatic tact. But now the diplomacy was being challenged by the fast food franchise owner.

"We *do* need a restaurant of some kind here," Grant admitted. "The one in the hotel won't be able to accommodate much more than their own guests... and it *is* a long walk between the hotel and the theater."

Keith pondered a moment. "What if you tell them *I'll* design their building, and *no golden arches outside?*"

"Why don't I just tell them no? That Russell Abbey has already made an offer on that lot."

Both Keith and Grant perked up. "You're kidding! Abbey's gonna put a restaurant out here?"

"I told him I'd have to clear it with the two of you first, but yeah, Russell wants to build here—maybe not as big as the place in Wellington, but the same quality."

"That's great! Abbey's in Silver Spring," Keith beamed. "Then we won't have to drive into town for a decent hamburger. When is he ready to go?"

"As soon as you can draw him some blueprints and get him some construction quotes."

"You got a sales contract ready for him?"

"I can have it ready Monday afternoon."

"Then I'll go there for lunch today... talk to him then," Keith said. "Anyone else wanna go to Abbey's for lunch?"

"Can't," Robin replied. "I promised Tanya I'd take her shopping today."

"And Christy is making lasagna... she'd kill me if I skipped out on that," Grant lamented.

"Suit yourselves," Keith said. "I'll dine alone."

Now that Grant was married and Robby could just as well be, Christy and Tanya had their way of occasionally separating the boys, inducement that was rarely possible before. Nothing short of death could possibly diminish the close friendship that Keith, Robby, and Grant had known since childhood. But it left Keith feeling like the fifth wheel sometimes, perhaps a little resentful. But he had adjusted accordingly; fond of his bachelor lifestyle, he intended to retain it for a long time to come.

"You could wait until Monday to see Russell," Grant suggested. "And you could join me and Christy for lasagna."

Keith thought a moment. "No, that's okay," he replied. "I appreciate the invitation, but I'm going into Wellington today anyway."

"Have either of you heard how the ticket sales are going for the next shows?" Robin asked. Although the Crystal Palace had its own business manager, it still remained under the boys' control—its revenue intended to sustain an adequate level of maintenance funds for the rest of the community.

"Last I heard," Grant said, "The Night Riders next weekend could be doing better, but the Shakespeare play the following weekend is nearly sold out already."

"The Night Riders have always filled the house without advance sales," Robin said. "Should we book the theater group for a couple more shows?"

"Wouldn't hurt... we've got a few open nights."

"I'll talk to Virgil," Keith said. "If he knows it's a sell-out, I'd bet he'll be eager to go a few more nights."

"Will the hotel be open by then?"

"A week from next Friday," Keith replied. "Right on schedule..."

And so went another of their early morning meetings discussing all the current affairs revolving around Silver Spring. These meetings, at one time, had endured an entire day, back when Silver Spring was in its embryo stages, when they believed their plan of reviving the ghost town really meant something, like setting a plow into the earth. Now they no longer feared that their efforts would be considered insignificant, as the public eye had taken serious notice of the mark they had scribed. So now, the morning meetings could sometimes be relatively brief; progress seemed to continue on its own momentum.

C hristy attributed her frightful morning headache to the four glasses of wine she had consumed the previous night— before, during, and after dinner. She and Grant had met some of her old friends in Wellington to celebrate a birthday.

She found Grant in his downstairs office analyzing a computer programming problem that had been submitted to him from a California based client. He hadn't planned to work that day; Saturdays were usually days when he could get away with not answering his phone unless he knew the call wasn't business related. But this was Mandarin & Company, a client that had been with him since the very beginning, and he felt somewhat obligated to devote his attention to their predicament.

"Why are you working?" Christy asked. "It's Saturday."

"Just wanted to get a jump on Monday, and I didn't want to disturb your rest. How's your headache?"

"I heard voices in the middle of the night. Did you hear them?" Christy asked.

"Are you sure you weren't dreaming?" Grant said. "Or maybe it was the wine."

Christy was clearly upset. She gently sat down in a chair with the tips of her fingers pressed against her temples. "I wasn't dreaming, and it wasn't the wine. I was wide awake. I got up to get some aspirin and a glass of water, and that's when I heard the voices."

"And you're sure it wasn't Robin and Tanya you

heard?"

"I'M SURE! Why don't you believe me? We've all heard them before."

"Okay... I believe you." Grant was satisfied that Christy had heard the voices. They hadn't been heard for a while, or the piano music or any other haunting indicators that the building supported some paranormal qualities. Robin Gladstone was certain that the ghosts occupying the old structure were harmless, that they were actually pleased with their new housemates. Most of the time he was quite convincing to everyone, constantly reminding his companions that nothing detrimental to the safety of any of the current *living* residents had ever occurred, that no one had ever experienced any injurious activity.

But the spirits were there. Everyone knew it. Although certain identity had never been established, it was assumed that the ghosts were those of the original hotel proprietor, Jeremiah Crane, probably his wife, Millie, and possibly some of the hotel's nineteenth century servant staff— maids, cooks, porters, and the like—and without a doubt, Alexander "Fingers" Malone *had* to be responsible for the sound of piano serenades at all hours of the day or night. He had been the main source of entertainment in the hotel during its glory years, and he had remained at the lodge right to the end.

Of course, there was always the possibility of less friendly spirits showing up; Silver Spring's history wasn't all apple blossoms, gingerbread and lace curtains. It had its share of roughness, too, and it had certainly seen plenty of outlaws—gunslingers, thieves, killers—all the usual mean critters that roamed the territory during the boom times. They left in their wake a trail of violence and bloodshed, and often they, too, became the victims of violent retaliation.

So far, though, the *new* Silver Spring had not been revisited by any of those undesirables. Christy, especially, was hopeful that *all* the specters would get bored with the world of the living and just move on. She was the only one uneasy about sharing this space with invisible entities, regardless that they seemed harmless.

Grant pushed away from his desk, walked the few steps to his wife, and kneeled beside her, caressing her silky dark hair. "I wish you weren't so afraid of them," he said with a consoling voice.

"It's not that I'm afraid of them," Christy returned. "It's just that I feel like... like there's someone watching us all the time."

Grant had not been skeptical of Christy's ghostly experience; he was simply being cautious and protective, as he was fully aware of her discomfort. But even though Tanglewood's ghostly encounters had recently remained somewhat inactive, other places around town were attracting some attention with increased spirit visitation. Curious and unexplained incidents were occurring with little regularity on the streets and in several of the replica store buildings: lights were already turned on upon early morning store openings; the sounds of doors opening and closing were occasionally heard, but when investigated, no one was there; actors of the theater troupe complained of missing props and other stage furnishings, only to find them later in strange places.

Yes, the ghosts of old Silver Spring were making their presence known, not in a malevolent manner, but more in a playful, mischievous way, and with enough frequency that some of the store operators were giving them names.

In the large building across from the Crystal Palace Theater where once stood the Royal Hotel & Saloon were now a bakery, a candy store, and a gift shop. Sounds of tinkling glasses and laughter could be heard occasionally, and sometimes the lights would be found burning in the morning. Everyone suspected that it must be the bartender from the Royal Saloon keeping the late-night hours. They called him Sam.

Light tapping noises emitted from somewhere within the T-Shirt shop just up the street. Tom's Boot Repair had occupied that corner in the 1890s, so it was supposed that Tom, the cobbler, was still there re-soling boots and shoes.

The prankster that kept moving props at the Crystal Palace could have been any number of nineteenth century actors or stage hands. But it seemed fitting that he be called Simon—after the original theater's owner, Simon Bordeaux.

Although Grant was intrigued by all this, as were his partners, Robin Gladstone and Keith Bradley, he tried to keep the information from becoming everyday conversation whenever Christy was around. It always swung her mood the wrong way.

I t was going to be a busy day for Keith after all; he'd thought about spending a lazy day—maybe fishing, or tinkering with his old classic car, the 1964 *El Camino* that he had acquired while he was in Colorado— but now there seemed to be things to do. While he waited for the theater rehearsal to wind down, he went to his office to search through the numerous sketches of old Silver Spring storefronts to show Russell Abbey. He sincerely hoped that Russell had been made aware of the exterior appearance regulation. As soon as Russell provided him with specifics regarding his layout requirements, Keith could start the designing process.

He put six prints of storefront designs in a folder, placed the folder in his briefcase, and headed for the rear entrance of Tanglewood, outside of which his car was waiting in their private six-car garage that appropriately resembled the old hotel's original stable and carriage house. A wooden privacy fence spanned between the two buildings, in front of which was the grave of the original hotel owner and its stone marker surrounded by a sturdy white picket fence.

Keith tossed his briefcase onto the back seat of his *Grand Prix.* He still drove the car that his dad had given him as a high school graduation gift; he loved that car and wouldn't think of giving it up. He gazed around the garage to the other vehicles: Robby still had the yellow *Mustang* convertible given to him at the same time, although it was now just a second car, the first being a late model *Lexus* sedan. Grant's *Jeep* had been replaced by a *Tahoe,* and his brother, Kevin, had inherited the *Jeep Wrangler.* Keith's classic *El Camino* occupied a stall in the carriage house, too. Quite a fleet.

The back side of the building housed a utility tractor, lawn mowers, a pickup truck, and a work shop where Kevin headquartered his staff of part-time maintenance helpers. Keith thought he would find Kevin there; perhaps Kevin would join him for lunch at Abbey's.

No Kevin. He walked briskly to the Crystal Palace where he intended to wait for an opportunity to talk with Virgil Thurston about running the Shakespeare play a few more nights than originally planned. Virgil was the sort of person who tolerated interruptions from no one, an attribute he had established years ago as an English Literature teacher at Wellington High. Now, well into his sixties, he was the renowned coach and director for the amateur theatrical troupe, and had been instrumental in arranging for stage time at the Crystal Palace. Even though Keith had known Virgil since his high school days in Virgil's classroom, he dared not intervene during a rehearsal. He knew better.

Just inside the front entrance of the theater Kevin stood with paint brush in hand, a pail of paint at his feet. "Hey, Keith," he greeted.

"Kevin," Keith responded. "You're at it pretty early today."

"Yeah... a lot to do here before next weekend."

"Wanna go to Abbey's for lunch today?"

Kevin stopped his brush strokes and stared at Keith a brief moment, that desire for the most tantalizing burger gleaming from his eyes. But then, as if conceding to a rival thought, he resumed the painting and said, "Better not. As much as I'd like to. Christy insisted that I have some of her lasagna."

"What? Don't you like her lasagna?"

"It's okay, I guess. It's just that... I think she's feeling a little hurt since I sorta moved in with you for the summer."

"Why would she feel hurt about that?"

"Don't know. Maybe my brother has something to do with it... thinks I should've moved in with them."

"So... why didn't you?"

Kevin stopped painting again and looked at Keith in near desperation. "Tell me, Keith. Would you want to live in the same apartment with your sister and her husband for a whole summer?"

Keith hesitated a moment, a vision of his most recent visit to his married older sister in San Francisco flashing before him. "Well... I don't know... I guess... it would de-pend..." And then it was as if he had been slapped by the God of Good Sense. *"No... I wouldn't...* come to think of it."

"Bingo!"

Keith had learned to like Kevin a lot more now than he had as a youngster—not that he disliked Kevin then, but Grant's little brother, five years younger, had always leaned on Robby Gladstone more than Grant. Robby had always been more tolerant of the little brother; the two of them seemed to blend together harmoniously, and their person-ality colors didn't clash. As of late, however, Kevin had felt the loss of closeness since Robby and Tanya had become one. Keith sympathized with Kevin, because not only had Kevin lost his intimate connection with the three older boys through Robby, he had lost the connection with his brother, albeit a bit corroded, when Grant and Christy tied the knot.

Kevin was the sort of son who pleased his father. He had been the captain of his high school soccer team. On the surface his manners were good, nurtured by sound training rather than strict discipline. His sights were set on gaining his teaching degree after one more year at the University, and perhaps settling into a high school coaching position somewhere. Flights of fantasy or sieges of longing never coaxed him from the present. He hadn't invented another life; the one he had seemed to suit him just fine. Yet he throbbed with the eagerness to contend, to be noticed, to be right, to win, to make others follow his lead; maybe a little cocky, but he wasn't one of those suave, self-conscious country club boys. He kept himself moderately well-groomed, but he thought little about such things—he wore un-ironed clothes right out of the dryer until they were dirty and his mom tossed them back into the washer.

Kevin had been awarded the same opportunity of a summer with minimal responsibility preceding his first year of college. By that time, though, the other boys— Robby, Grant, and Keith—had returned and were already engaged in the Silver Spring project. Their adventure of four years previous would have been difficult to top; as their legacy, Kevin chose to remain associated with them, to remain the small part of the adventure he had once been. And each summer break since, he returned to work and to be with them here. It just seemed natural.

They could hear from beyond the inner doors to the auditorium the raised voice of Virgil Thurston barking out directives to the actors for preparation of the next rehearsal, and asking for volunteers to help with finishing touches on the stage sets.

"Sounds like practice is over," Keith said. "I have to talk with Virgil... catch up to you later."

The array of players had dispersed from the stage and were emerging out the side doors like drone bees from a hive. Mr. Thurston leaned against the stage front pondering over a loose leaf notebook, scribbling notations. He was a man of tweed sport coats, correct speech, sensible stock options, a practiced interest in knowledge and an obsessive interest in sports, especially the muddy, dangerous ones like football and hockey that ended with hulks hobbling off the field to have their battle wounds tended to at the sidelines, knees and elbows scarred, hair matted with sweat, and war-like streaks of mud daubed across red, overheated faces.

He looked up to see Keith approaching. "Good morning, Mr. Bradley," he said.

"Good morning," Keith responded. "How was rehearsal?"

"Considering that we still have two weeks to iron out a few difficulties, I guess you could say that it went well."

"Difficulties? Anything we can do to help?"

"Oh, no... the difficulty I'm referring to, my good man, is that of actors not understanding the brilliance of Shakespeare."

Keith chuckled. "I can relate to that."

"Yes... well, we'll work it out. Of what do I owe the pleasure of your visit, Mr. Bradley?"

"My partners and I were discussing this morning the possibility of running your play a few more nights. You *are aware* that all three performances are nearly sold out, aren't you?"

"Yes, I had heard such rumors."

"It's no rumor, Virgil. The new hotel will be open by then, too, and I'm sure some of the guests would appreciate a little entertainment, not to mention the locals who've not gotten their tickets yet."

"I'll take it into consideration... and of course, the cast will have to be in favor of an extended run."

"Of course. You can contact Marcia, the theater manger... so we can print more tickets."

Kevin continued his painting of the interior woodwork trim around the doors. With all three of the front entrance doors propped open for plenty of ventilation, he could periodically glance out on Main Street and see the activity there. This early in the morning, there still weren't a lot of people yet; only a few cars were parked in the Market Square, and a few early-riser tourists sauntered about, browsing the shop windows, clicking snapshots of their noisy children posing in front of the vintage storefronts holding yappy, curious little dogs at the end of leashes. Everything was bathed in morning sunshine, although high towers of clouds rolled steadily closer from the west like war machines invading the vast blue sky empire. Rain was likely within a few hours.

Across the street the aroma of fresh-baked bread, cinnamon rolls and chocolate chip cookies lured several people into the new bakery; it was always the first shop to open in the morning, offering not only the tempting baked goods, but coffee and other beverages as well. It was the closest semblance to a restaurant in Silver Spring so far, and in a very short time it had become a popular spot. The six café tables on its front verandah filled quickly.

Among the small crowd feasting on warm cinnamon rolls, apple fritters, coffee and orange juice, Kevin noticed a young man that he had seen several times before—unusual because most of the people who visited Silver Spring, unless they were locals from Wellington or the immediate area, were usually tourists just passing through, so the faces changed nearly every hour of every day. This fellow, though, didn't appear to be a tourist, but Kevin didn't think he was a local resident, either; a college student, perhaps, but the small college campus at Wellington was deserted for the summer. He wasn't in costume, so it was doubtful that he belonged to the theater group portraying Silver Spring ghosts. His physical build suggested an athlete; his graceful motions hinted a ballet dancer.

He politely waved other patrons to enter the bakery ahead of him, and as he waited for the crowded little store to clear, he pulled a few small weeds from the brightly flowered planter box at the outer edge of the verandah and pruned some dry leaves from the geraniums, caressing and grooming, as if he were the lord and keeper of this, his own private plot. Kevin's curiosity was getting the better of him; it was time for a cup of coffee from the bakery, but more importantly, he felt the urge to get a closer look at the self-appointed flower box caretaker.

By the time Kevin had pressed the lid on the paint pail and strolled across the street, the young man emerged from the bakery with a white paper bag and a large Styrofoam cup. But the cup didn't contain coffee or orange juice; it held water that he carefully dispensed into the flower box, distributing it evenly among the many plants.

"That probably isn't necessary," Kevin said as he approached. He pointed skyward. "Gonna rain in a little while."

The mystery guest gazed for a moment up to the sky; from his vantage point, he saw only clear blue, as the building was blocking his view of the storm clouds slowly approaching from the west. "Guess I didn't notice... they looked a little dry—"

"I didn't get 'round to watering the flowers yet," Kevin interrupted. "Been busy with other stuff."

Slightly embarrassed, as if he'd been caught doing something he shouldn't, the young man glanced at Kevin, then the open theater doors, then back to Kevin. "You work here... you're the painter... I'm sorry... I just thought the flowers needed a little water and—"

"It's okay," Kevin said. He held out his right hand. "I'm Kevin, and yes, I work here during the summer, and I really don't mind that you water the flowers."

"Jerry," the fellow responded as he clumsily shifted the empty cup to his left hand that was holding the paper bag. Relieved that Kevin wasn't there to chastise him for unauthorized care of the foliage, he smiled and accepted the handshake.

"Welcome to Silver Spring, Jerry," Kevin said.

"Thanks. I saw the signs out on the highway, and then I heard some people in town talking about the place... thought I'd check it out."

"So what d'ya think?"

"Well, honestly, I expected to see a modern, glass-walled gift shop selling maps for self-guided walking tours around a bunch of decaying old buildings, you know, caved in or in various stages of falling down..."

"Are you disappointed?"

"Oh, no! Not in the least. It's just not your average ghost town... if there's such a thing as an *average* ghost town."

"No, I guess it isn't average," Kevin replied. "Now that your cup is empty, can I get you a coffee? I was just on my way in to get one."

"Thanks, but I don't usually drink coffee."

"Something else? Orange juice... Coke..."

"A Coke would be good."

They went inside to get the drinks. When they returned to the verandah, Kevin directed the visitor to sit at one of the two tables that had been vacated. "I've seen you here several times in the past few days," he said. "You live around here?"

"No... well... sort of."

Kevin eyed Jerry questioningly.

"I'm camping... about a mile from here. They said in town that it would be okay."

"As long as you're not on someone's private property."

"I backpacked into to hills... where they told me. Is this *really* a ghost town?" Jerry changed the subject. "All these buildings look new."

"Genuine. When my brother and his friends found this place it was only a field of stone foundations... and the old hotel." Kevin pointed and nodded toward Tanglewood. "It was the only building left intact."

"What happened to the rest of the town?"

"Burned to the ground... eighteen-ninety-nine. The ruins of the silver smelter are just down the hill... at the far end of the parking lot." Kevin pointed again toward the new Silver Spring Hotel.

"So this was a mining town?"

"Yeah... it has quite an interesting history. It's just not famous and well-known like Deadwood or Tombstone."

"I'd like to hear it... or read it. Is there a book?"

"The only book that tells the true story about Silver Spring isn't likely to leave the vault at Tanglewood." Kevin pointed again. "And I really don't have time right now. I should be getting back to work."

"Painting?"

"Yeah… among other things. There's a lot to do before the theater re-opens next weekend."

An expression of loneliness more than disappointment washed over Jerry's face. "Oh, yeah, you're busy. I shouldn't be bothering you."

"Gonna be around for a while? I could meet you again later… when I get done this afternoon."

"Sure… that would be great."

7

E ven with the amount of work that needed to get done, at three o'clock Kevin thought he had put in enough time for a Saturday. The rain had stopped; he put away his tools and headed for Tanglewood; a cool shower and clean clothes were in order.

"Still have time to talk?" a voice called out.

Kevin looked around. There was Jerry strolling toward him from across the street, backpack in hand and looking eager for social activity. He had remained scarce since their meeting that morning.

"Sure," Kevin returned. "Just wanna get a shower and some clean clothes first... okay?"

"I'll just wait around here, then," Jerry said.

Then Kevin remembered that Jerry said he was camping out in the wilderness. He probably didn't have anywhere else to go. "You can wait in the reception room if you'd like... one of our *genuine* historic highlights."

Jerry accepted the invitation, threw his pack over his shoulder and started walking with Kevin.

"So what've you been doing all day?" Kevin asked.

"Checked out the smelter ruins on the hill, had a nice bath in the creek, and then sat on the verandah under the roof and read while it was raining."

"What were you reading?"

"David Copperfield."

"Oh yeah? I read that in English Lit in high school... loved it."

"Yeah, I read it back then, too, but I think I'm enjoying it more now."

As they approached Tanglewood, Jerry started to notice the grandness of the huge old structure. Even a youngster like Jerry could recognize its significance. Its tan bricks—on the color spectrum somewhere between buckskin and butterscotch—spoke of age, not in a decrepit and withered sense, but more of majestic wisdom. Forty-some feet across its front and more than a hundred feet long, towering two stories—three by modern dimensional standards—its mere size seemed a frontier architectural wonder. It suggested grandeur of a time gone by, only imaginable at present, preserved in its monolithic, yet exquisite fortitude. Surviving when all else around it crumbled, protected by an unseen entity, the grand old hotel remained as a stately monument, undaunted by the challenges of time.

"This is where you live?" Jerry asked.

"Yeah," Kevin replied. He pointed to the upper level behind a broad deck that also served as the canopy over the lower veranda extending the full breadth of the building. "Three apartments upstairs and offices for my brother and his partners downstairs. It's all quite modern except for this."

They entered the front door.

"Wow!" Jerry exclaimed when he gazed around the restored saloon. "You weren't kidding about the historical highlight." His eyes fell on the authentic antique furnishings around the room, the cast-iron stove, the upright piano, the original mahogany bar and back bar complete with old, corked brown whiskey bottles lined up in front of a large wall mirror.

"This is the only part they left like this," Kevin explained. "Make yourself comfortable. I'll be down in a little while." He dashed up the grand staircase that led to a small balcony in front of Keith's apartment door and let himself in. Keith had not yet returned from Wellington.

When he got out of the shower he could hear the tinkling of the piano below him; whoever was playing it seemed quite talented. *Whoever?* This was quite unusual. Now that Tanglewood was occupied most of the time, the 3:15 piano music hadn't been heard in quite some time... *and it was about 3:15.* There was no one down in the saloon except Jerry, and Jerry hadn't been warned about the building being haunted.

Kevin quickly toweled himself dry, but before he could get to his clothes, he heard a scream and the sound of the piano suddenly stopped. He recognized the voice, now, that had also produced the scream. It was Christy. "Who are you?" she was yelling frantically. Kevin knew she had to have come through the door from the offices into the saloon and encountered the visitor. She had always been a little uneasy about living in a haunted house, and Kevin could understand how terrified she might be coming face-to-face with an uninvited stranger. He wrapped the towel around his waist and headed for the stairway as quickly as possible. The screams and yelling continued. Half-way down he saw Jerry standing in the middle of the room with an expression of terror on his face, staring at Christy at the interior door with an equally terrified look.

"It's okay, Christy," Kevin said, trying to calm her down before the situation got any more out of control. He ran down the rest of the steps and positioned himself between the two would-be combatants. "It's okay," he said again, reassuring Christy that there was nothing to be upset about.

"I heard the piano," she cried, "And I thought..." She seemed quite upset and couldn't finish her statement.

Kevin eyed Jerry again. "Who was playing the piano?" he asked. "Were *you* playing the piano?"

"I'm sorry," Jerry whimpered. "I didn't think it would hurt. I'm really sorry."

Just then Grant came rushing through the office door. "I heard screaming! What's going on here?" He gave an astonished glance at Kevin wearing nothing but a bath towel and then stared past him to the stranger. "Who are you?"

"I'm Jerry Stevens. I—"

"What are you doing here?" Grant questioned. Christy threw her arms around him as if she were seeking protection from some horrible monster.

Kevin intervened. "He was waiting for *me* while I was taking a shower, and he played the piano."

"Oh, so you know this gentleman?"

"Yes," Kevin lied. This was the first time he'd even heard Jerry's last name. But he didn't think Jerry Stevens deserved the harsh treatment he was getting. "He wanted to know about Silver Spring and we were gonna hang out for a while."

Grant softened a little, like he usually did when the circumstances obviously seemed to be less threatening than they first appeared. "Well, then... I guess there's no harm done." He turned to Christy. "It's okay, honey... really. He's a friend of Kevin's." Then he extended his right hand toward Jerry. "I'm Kevin's brother, Grant." He smiled as if amused by the incident. "And you've already had the pleasure to meet my wife, Christy."

Jerry accepted the handshake, although he seemed a bit shaken by what had just happened. "Sorry for the disturbance, ma'am," he apologized. "I really didn't mean to—"

"That's okay... no harm done," Grant said. "We used to get a little jumpy when we heard piano music and there was no one playing the piano. Hasn't happened in a while."

Jerry glanced quickly at the old upright, and then back to Grant. "No one playing..." his voice trailed off, sounding a bit confused.

"I'm sure Kevin will explain it to you," Grant said, and then he stared with a smirk at his brother for a long moment. "Kev," he said calmly. "You should really get some clothes on if you're going to entertain guests." He turned and guided Christy out of the saloon and the door closed behind them.

"I'm really sorry," Jerry said again. "I didn't mean to cause trouble."

"Don't worry 'bout it," Kevin replied. "She kinda over-reacts sometimes. Let me get dressed and then I'll try to explain all this to you."

C lad in wrinkled cotton shirt and knee-length shorts right out of the dryer, Kevin plodded down the stairs, combing his fingers through his semi-dried hair. A fashion statement, he was not; the only features matching about his shirt and shorts were the wrinkles. But he wasn't too concerned about that.

"Okay..." he said as he reached the saloon floor and sat on a wooden chair beside Jerry. "You're built like an athlete; you move like a ballet dancer; you have a green thumb; and you play the piano. Anything else? Do you perform brain surgery during the week?"

Jerry laughed. "No... but I'll give you an A for perception."

"So you *are* a footballer *and* a ballet dancer."

Jerry laughed again. "I wrestled in high school, and I'm a black belt tae kwon do... requires a lot of, shall we say, graceful balance."

"I'm impressed," Kevin responded.

"And I'd peg you as a soccer player," Jerry said.

"Well, you get an A *plus*. I've been playing footy since I was eight. What are you? Psychic, too?"

"I really don't know what I am, Kevin. Tell me... what did your brother mean about the piano music when there's no one playing the piano?" He obviously was redirecting the spotlight of the conversation away from himself.

"Oh. That," Kevin replied. "Well, this building is haunted. We used to hear piano music and voices, but not so much anymore. Muffled voices, sometimes, but no piano for a long time, now."

"How many live here?"

"Six... if you count me. I'm just here summers."

"One of the six messin' with the rest of you?"

"I assure you, Jerry, no one living here knows how to play the piano... not like that."

"Like what?"

"Old time... honky tonk... like you hear in the Western movies. You see, this place dates back to the eighteen-eighties and nineties. Silver Spring was kind of a rough town, and right at the last, the owner of this hotel was gunned down right here in this room. The guy who shot him set the rest of the town on fire trying to get away, and then the hotel owner's brother killed him right out in front... clubbed him with a burning beam."

"Wow!" Jerry replied. "Now I see why you said this place has an interesting history."

"Yeah, well, the really interesting part is what my brother and his partners discovered here."

"What was that?"

"Robby's grandfather was the newspaper editor in Wellington years ago... he had stashed an old journal in their attic... written by this hotel owner's brother and there were clues in that journal to a hidden treasure out here that nobody had ever found. Actually, nobody dared come here to look for it 'cause everybody knew the place was haunted and thought it was dangerous."

"So, what was the treasure?"

"Seventy-pound gold and silver ingots... a lot of 'em."

"You're kidding, right?"

"No. Swear to God. I saw 'em... well, some of them. And I found over eight thousand dollars worth of old coins, right here in this building."

"Really?"

"Yeah… one mint condition silver dollar was worth over five thousand."

"Where was the gold and silver?"

"In an old abandoned mine shaft, and because of a landslide it was well hidden and almost impossible to get at. Some guy who worked in the smelter was stealing 'em and stashing 'em in there, but he got caught and was killed in a shootout and nobody ever knew about the bars he had been hiding in the mine shaft."

"And your brother found it."

"Yeah, and Robby and Keith—his two partners. Then they went off to college for four years, and when they came back, gold and silver prices went through the roof. They bought all this land and started rebuilding the town."

"Why did they want to do that?"

"Because they'd fallen in love with the place… and they had the money to do it."

"That explains why all the buildings look new."

"But they're trying to keep it looking authentic. Keith's a really good architect and he's the one who designed it all."

"And your share in all this?"

"My share was the old coins I found."

"And they *let* you work here summers."

"Yeah… I'll get my teaching degree next year, but I'll probably still come back here summers… I think I've fallen in love with the place, too. There's something so mysterious and magical about it."

A furry gray creature came slinking down in the shadows on the stairway. Jerry caught a glimpse when it stopped midway and peered at him from between the banister spindles.

"Who's that?" Jerry curiously asked.

Kevin turned to look where Jerry was looking. "Oh, that's Munchkin," and then he called out to the cat. "Hello, Munchkin."

On hearing his name, the feline trotted down the rest of the steps and abruptly appeared at Kevin's feet, scrutinizing the visitor. "Mrrraow," he said, and then cautiously padded to Jerry's feet, sniffing his sneakers.

"They should've called him Sherlock," Kevin mused. "He's quite the detective... curious about everything and doesn't miss anything." He leaned down and scratched Munchkin between his ears. "Where's Rocky and Zeus?" he asked the cat, as if he expected an answer.

The cat looked toward the office door just momentarily, and then went back to investigating the hair on Jerry's legs.

Jerry leaned down to pet the cat; Munchkin immediately started to purr, absorbing the attention. "Who are Rocky and Zeus?" Jerry asked.

"Two more cats, but they rarely come in here... they don't seem to like this room like Munchkin does."

A few moments went by and then Kevin asked, "So what about you, Jerry?"

"What about me?"

"Yeah, you. I know you're not from around here, but you're not the typical tourist, either."

"You don't want to know about me."

"Sure I do. Why wouldn't I?"

Jerry straightened up, left Munchkin purring at his feet. Elbows on knees and fingertips forming a teepee at his chin, he puzzled Kevin: "To be perfectly honest with you,

Kevin, even I don't know who or what I am."

"What do you mean?"

Jerry hesitated a moment. "I don't know how to explain it without sounding like some sort of loser bum."

"I'm pretty understanding," Kevin replied. "Try me."

"I've been no more than a drifter for the last couple of years; my folks couldn't tolerate the person I'd become, and I knew I'd already caused them enough grief, so I just left... thought I'd try to get myself straightened out again."

"What have you been doing all that time?"

"Going from place to place, working for a while, then moving on."

"Are you working anyplace now?"

"I *was* working with a construction crew, but when their last job was finished, I didn't go back for the next one."

"So... what are you gonna do now?"

"Don't know... maybe I should just go away... lose myself in the woods and stay there until my memory comes back and I know who I am."

"Your memory? What d'ya mean?"

"That's the problem, Kevin. There are parts of my life missing... in my head... and I don't know who or what I was before the..." He abruptly stopped short.

"Before what?"

Jerry gazed down at the floor. "I shouldn't be laying all this on a total stranger... I'm sorry."

"Jerry Stevens," Kevin said. "A stranger is a friend you haven't met yet... and we've already met, so we're certainly not strangers. And from what I'm sensing, I'd say *you* need a friend. *Everyone* needs a friend in this life... someone who you can take a chance on the truth."

"But I don't really know you, Kevin, no offense, nor do

you really know me."

"Okay," Kevin said. He took a deep breath. "My full name is Kevin Alan Kraemer; I'm twenty-one years old; I got lucky and was born into a good family; my father is an electrical engineer; I graduated with honors from Wellington High three years ago; I was the captain of the soccer team; I'm single and don't have a girlfriend; next year I'll get my teaching degree from the university and I want to be a soccer coach.

"There. You know all about me. What else do you require that will make you know you can trust me?"

"Thank you for wanting to be a friend," Jerry said. "You've been very kind. But neither of us knows what I was, or what I will be if I should return to my old self."

"Then make a decision to start over. No matter what you've been, you can always become something else."

Jerry contemplated that for a few moments. There was no anger in him, just concern. "Do you really think it's that simple? Is a person ruled by his own free will? Or is he ruled by all of his experiences, education and heredity? I may not know what I am, but my body does, and it reacts the way it has been conditioned to react... the habits conditioned into my muscles have forgotten nothing."

"Jerry," Kevin responded. "You're a nice guy; in the short time I've known you, listening to you talk, no matter *what* your past, I can't believe that you were a bad person."

A few minutes passed; neither of them spoke. Munchkin jumped up into Jerry's lap seeking more attention, and both took advantage of the diversion, petting and scratching the cat while they were both in deep thought. Kevin thought of how impressed he felt about Jerry's apparent intelligence; his clear and composed speech gave evidence that he was well educated, and if he really did possess a black belt in the martial arts, he had to be well focused. But what of this memory loss issue? Was it a cover-up for some sinister quality that would be better left alone? Kevin didn't want to believe that there could be such a dark side to Jerry.

Jerry thought about his next move. Should he continue to hide the real, painful story, what little he remembered? Or should he heed Kevin's sincere-sounding petition for friendship? True, he did not have many friends now since he left home, only acquaintances, and he had let none of them penetrate his inner secrets. But what the hell? He would probably be gone from here in a few days anyway; it wouldn't matter.

Jerry finally broke the silence. "My brother died in a car accident," he said solemnly. "And it was my fault... they said I was driving way too fast... lost control on a curve... went off the road and crashed into some trees. When I woke up the next morning in the hospital a doctor told me that I was lucky to come out of it with only a concussion. Of course, I knew it was more than just that 'cause I was pretty sore from other bumps and bruises, but I couldn't remember how I'd gotten them until he told me about the car wreck. And then he told me that my brother hadn't been so lucky."

Concerned astonishment washed over Kevin. "I'm sorry... I didn't mean to dredge up something agonizing."

"It's okay," Jerry said, thwarting any further apologies. "It was a long time ago... three years... and I've learned to live with the fact that I killed my brother... an *accident* they called it. And maybe it was, but it was still my fault."

"Look, Jerry, if you don't want to talk about it..."

"It's okay... really. Maybe it's good that I talk about it. You're the first person I've told this to in over two years."

"So a bad bump on the head from the accident gave you amnesia?"

"Not totally. At first, everyone thought it was quite natural that I was avoiding any conversation or thoughts about my brother, but then family—and friends—started acting really strangely toward me and I didn't know why... until they told me that I had become a different person, but I didn't know what they were talking about because I didn't know the person I had been before."

"Is that why you left?"

"My folks had lost one son, and they were having a hard time dealing with that, and they were taking it out on me, accusing me of not caring that Charles was gone, when in fact I didn't even remember him or any relationship I'd had with him. I couldn't stand it anymore, so I packed up and hit the road."

"You don't remember him at all?" Kevin asked.

"I know this sounds crazy to you. Maybe there's always the possibility that I have false memory syndrome, and none of this ever happened. Maybe I'm some other person completely and this whole thing is just a weird dream. Or maybe I'm the ghost of some dead guy who hasn't realized he's dead. But since I just pinched myself and I didn't wake up, I'll assume that it's not a dream and that it all did happen..."

The front door opened. Keith stepped inside. Dressed rather casually in jeans and golf shirt, he carried a briefcase, and on his face was the grin to end all grins. Munchkin leaped to the floor and dashed to him, stretching his paws up on Keith's leg. Keith scooped up the purring cat with his left hand. "Hello, Munchkin," he said, and the cat returned the greeting with a "Mrrraow."

"Hi, Keith," Kevin said from across the room.

"Hi, Kev. How's the painting coming along?"

"I should have it done in a couple more days."

"Who's your friend?" Keith casually walked across the room to where the two were sitting.

"Oh! This is Jerry Stevens. Jerry, this is Keith Bradley, my brother's business partner... our resident architect... and my summer roommate."

Jerry stood. "Pleased to meet you," he said as they shook hands. "Kevin's been telling me about the history of this place."

"I hope he didn't scare you," Keith mused.

"Oh, no... Grant's wife did the scaring."

Kevin intervened when he saw that Keith seemed a little confused. "She came in screaming when she heard Jerry playing the piano."

Too ecstatic with thoughts about his meeting with Russell Abbey and the new restaurant project, Keith accepted that as sufficient without any further explanation. "You guys might like to know," he said, "Abbey's running a special on Ranch Burgers today."

"How 'bout it?" Kevin asked his guest. "Want the best burger you ever ate in your life? I'll buy."

"I could use some help," Kevin proposed to the Monday morning meeting in the saloon. He wasn't usually present at these meetings, but he had a purpose. "With the theater painting project, I'm getting a little behind with other things. I'd like to hire someone... if it's okay with you."

Robin, Grant and Keith exchanged puzzled stares. "Since when do you need our approval to hire a helper?" Grant asked. "Got any applicants?"

"Yes, as a matter of fact, I do."

"Would it be that fellow I saw you with in here on Saturday?" Keith asked.

Kevin nodded. "Yeah. I had a long talk with him at Abbey's... seems to be a really good guy, and he could use a job for the summer."

"Jerry? Was that his name? Is he from around here?"

"No... Chicago."

"Oh!" Grant said. "The guy who scared the crap out of Christy?"

"Yeah," Kevin said. "Does that disqualify him?"

"No... actually, we had a good laugh about it when we got back upstairs."

"Actually," Kevin replied. "I think Christy scared Jerry

more than he scared her."

"What and who are you guys talking about?" Robin asked. He was the only one who had not yet met Jerry.

"Jerry Stevens," Kevin started to explain. "He was playing the piano Saturday afternoon. Guess Christy got a little unnerved and came running in screaming."

"What was he doing in here in the first place?"

"I was upstairs taking a shower... he was waiting for me."

"You knew this guy?"

"I do now," Kevin said. "He's staying in the area and he wouldn't mind working here for the rest of the summer. He's already been taking care of the planter boxes on Main Street voluntarily."

"I was wondering about that," Robin said. "I noticed them yesterday, and I thought maybe you had finally gained some gardening techniques." He playfully punched Kevin's arm. "They look quite presentable."

"Jerry seemed a little on edge," Keith said. "Like he was disturbed about something."

Kevin's face turned somber. "We had just been talking... before you came in. Jerry's younger brother was killed in a car wreck, and he's kinda messed up over it... thinks it was his fault. And his family is down on him about it, too, so that's why he's here... needs to be around friends who aren't gonna keep reminding him about it."

"Well," Robin said, attempting to brighten up the room again. "If Jerry can do anything else as good as he does the flower planters, then you won't hear any objections from me. Just have him fill out the necessary paperwork so we can pay him."

Kevin had completed his mission; there was no reason

for him to stay any longer. "Okay then... guess I'll get back to my painting."

When Jerry came into the theater lobby, Kevin hadn't painted a stroke; he was still searching for his paint brushes that he was certain he had left right next to the paint cans. The cans were lined up neatly along the wall next to the ticket booth, but the brushes were nowhere in sight.

"Morning," Jerry said.

Kevin acknowledged. "Morning," he replied over his shoulder from the far side of the room. "It seems that I have misplaced my paint brushes. I'm sure that I left them right there with the paint cans Saturday afternoon, but they're gone now."

"Ghosts," Jerry said jokingly. "Maybe you have ghosts in here." It was a common spontaneous response that most people would express. Jerry didn't give any thought to, nor did he know anything of the actual circumstances.

Kevin turned toward Jerry and eyed him with a curious grin. "Yes... it could be Simon, I guess."

"Who's Simon?"

Kevin stepped casually back to where Jerry was standing by the ticket booth. "Remember when I told you about Tanglewood being haunted?"

"Yeah."

"Well... some other places around here seem to have acquired the presence of ghosts, too."

Jerry scanned the room with a sudden touch of fright in his eyes.

"Oh, but don't worry, Jerry," Kevin assured him. "All our ghosts—including Simon—are friendly. They don't hurt anybody... just talk about us and when we're not looking get into mischief once in a while... like hiding my paint brushes."

Jerry was just returning to a state of relief when the inner theater door burst open. Startled half out of their wits, both Jerry and Kevin spun around to face the door. To Jerry, the gray-haired man standing in the doorway holding three paint brushes could have been the ghost that Kevin just mentioned, but to Kevin, it was a familiar face.

"Oh! Hello, Mr. Thurston," Kevin greeted. "What are you doing here?"

"I'm meeting a few of the cast members to work on the set. Kevin... did you leave these brushes on the stage? They appear to have the same gold color stained in the bristles that you are using out here."

Kevin stared at the brushes in Virgil's hand. "They certainly look like mine." He sauntered over to the director and accepted the three different sized brushes. "Where did you say you found them?"

"On the stage, but they didn't look like anything we were using to paint the set, so I thought they might be yours."

"I didn't put them there—"

"Simon," said Mr. Thurston. He winked and turned to go back to the stage. "Simon!" he called out as he walked to the front of the theater. "You're at it again!"

Kevin gave a devilish grin as he turned to Jerry. "See? Nothing to be afraid of."

"Who... who was that?" Jerry asked in a bit of a daze.

"Virgil Thurston. He's the director for the Wellington theatrical club. They've performed here several times. Their new play opens in a couple of weeks."

"What play?"

Kevin pointed to a large, elegantly-framed poster on

the wall. Jerry studied it for a moment.

"Midsummer Night's Dream… Shakespeare… I love that play!"

"You've seen it before?"

"Oh, sure. I joined a drama club in college and auditioned for that play. I was chosen as an understudy, but I never got to perform on stage."

"College?" Kevin asked. "Where did you go to college?"

"Illinois… Northwestern." Then, as if to deliberately change the subject he said, "So did you talk to the owners about my employment here?"

"I did," Kevin replied. "When can you start?"

"Fifteen minutes ago. What should I do first?"

10

After his introduction to the equipment and tool room, Jerry needed very little supervision in the duties of grounds maintenance. Within a couple of days he had settled into a regimen of landscape manicure in such a style that anyone might have guessed he was a professional horticulturist and well-trained landscape artist. The property owners were quite pleased and impressed with his abilities and ambition, and now it was possible for Kevin to concentrate on his main project—the theater.

The number of cars in the theater parking lot each evening indicated that rehearsals were in full swing. One night, after working a little later than usual, Kevin slipped quietly into an aisle seat at the back of the auditorium to observe. The entire cast was on hand, carrying scripts and looking anything but Shakespearean players in their T-shirts, ragged cutoff shorts and sneakers. Director Thurston seemed in a rather foul mood as there was a little harshness in his voice.

"Theseus!" he called out to the actors on stage. "Take longer, more deliberate strides. You're a duke! You live in a palace! And Hermia... show some respect for your father but don't hide behind him! Now, let's try that entrance again... begin with 'Long live Theseus'..."

The players shuffled around on stage to their starting positions, and began the scene again.

Kevin could sense the tension, even from his back row seat; Virgil was certainly causing a level of uneasiness among the performers, but the reason wasn't yet clear. After they had tried to improve on the scene a half-dozen times or more, Thurston finally dismissed that group. "Okay," he said. "Let's skip to act two, scene one… Robin Goodfellow and the Fairy meet in the woods."

As the different group of actors took to the wings preparing for their entrance onto the stage, Kevin felt a hand lay heavily on his shoulder. Jerry urged him to move to the next seat so he could sit down. "I've been looking for you," he whispered.

"What's up?" Kevin replied.

"Did you eat yet? Thought maybe we could go somewhere for dinner."

"Sure. I just wanted to sit here and relax for a while. My back and shoulders ache from all this painting."

"I hauled up some neat landscaping rocks from the creek this afternoon… you'll have to check out the corner of the empty lot next to the theater."

"Okay… I'll look later…"

While they exchanged whispers about their day's work, Jerry's eyes remained focused on the stage as the rehearsal progressed, and the director continued to criticize the actors' efforts. "Oberon! Can you act more like a king and less like a mouse? And you, Titania… we're doing Shakespeare, not Alice in Wonderland. You're carrying your hands like a rabbit! And Robin… stop looking at your wristwatch! This is the sixteenth century!" None of this was said in good nature.

The actors looking on and waiting their turn for their scenes exchanged uneasy glances. Larry Johnson who was playing Hermia's father, Egeus, older than most of the others by at least fifteen years, a jeweler in Willington, was usually calm and mild-mannered, but now his eyes flashed a bit of anger, like a rattlesnake poked with a stick, and it could be seen even from the back row. Preston Gage who played the role of Robin Goodfellow—Puck, the merry and mischievous sprite—threw his script at Thurston and walked out. The whole auditorium fell into an eerie silence when the side door slammed shut.

Of all the actors in the cast, Preston Gage was Virgil Thurston's problematic gremlin. Just out of high school and somewhat a spoiled brat, Preston had an attitude and a temper, but there was no denying that he was a fairly good actor. On good days he could be charming and pleasant, a joy to be with on stage, eager to help a fellow performer with any dilemma. His striking good looks were admired by all the gals, and despised—or at least envied—by most of the guys. Charm combined with talent made excellent stage presence; Virgil considered Preston an asset to the group. But his disposition, at times, was quite unstable and unpredictable, and his highly emotional temper tantrums tended to be overpowering. This was one of those times.

Kevin wondered if the rest of the cast would follow; he wondered if *Midsummer Night's Dream* would ever open at all.

Then Jerry spoke up, a little louder this time: *"I'll put a girdle round about the earth in forty minutes."*

In the stillness of the cavernous room, his voice carried onto the stage. Everyone there recognized his words as the next line that Puck—Preston—should have recited. Thurston spun around to see who had intervened with such precise timing; his eyes fell on Kevin and Jerry in the back row, and then he turned back to address the actors on stage in a more civil tone. "Okay... let's go on. We can continue without Puck for now." He sounded as if he fully expected Preston to return once he had cooled down. But when King Oberon spoke the cue line for Puck to re-enter the scene, *"Welcome back traveler. Do you have the flower?"*... Preston was nowhere to be seen.

Another siege of tension gripped all the actors; they expected Mr. Thurston to erupt in another fit of rage. As they all turned their gaze to stage left from where Puck should have entered, Jerry spoke again, this time louder: *"Yes, I have the flower. Here it is."*

Once again, everyone including the director turned their astonished attention to the back of the theater, staring at Kevin and Jerry.

After a long moment of silence, Virgil called out: "KEVIN! Unless, after three years at University you have become well-versed in something other than soccer, I highly doubt that it was you correctly reciting lines from a Shakespearean play!"

"No. No, sir. It was not I," Kevin responded.

"Then, shall I assume it was your friend? Or should I consider the possibility that our resident ghost, *Simon* is rehearsing with us tonight?"

Kevin grinned. "Guess I'd put my money on Jerry, here, Mr. Thurston."

His response gained a few laughs and giggles from the cast; the serious weight that had been pressing on everyone seemed to lift and the tension dispersed.

"All right, everyone," Virgil announced. "Let's call it a night. Tomorrow at six p.m. sharp. We'll be working on act three. Learn your lines so you don't have to be constantly looking at the script."

If he could have the chance, Virgil Thurston would gladly relive the previous night's rehearsal, and he would live it differently the second time around. He deeply regretted the way he had treated the cast, and he sincerely hoped he could make it up to them somehow. Virgil didn't know why he had been in such a foul mood; nonetheless, one of the leading characters had walked off the set, and now he wasn't responding to Virgil's attempts at apology. Preston Gage had ignored his phone messages, and even his mother couldn't convince him to return the director's calls. At this late date, it would be difficult to find a replacement; it seemed to Virgil that *Midsummer Night's Dream* was doomed—or at least, subject to postponement—and there was no one to blame but himself. To make matters worse, he was so upset with himself that he wasn't thinking clearly.

Sometimes he wondered why he struggled with this ragtag bunch of amateurs. But quickly enough he would remember the answers: he loved the theater and he loved being a director; it was the best therapy to cure his loneliness since his wife's passing several years ago; it was the best way to occupy the time after his retirement from thirty-six years of teaching English Literature; it was gratifying to see the results of his efforts on opening night and every night after.

He had but one option right now: go to Marcia, the theater manager, and explain the situation. There was still enough time to make public announcements for an alternate opening date; all was not lost. Not yet.

"Good afternoon, Mr. Thurston," Kevin greeted the director from high on a stepladder. "Having an early rehearsal today?"

"No," Virgil replied. "Six o'clock as usual. Actually, I'm here to see Marcia. She hasn't left yet, has she?"

"Not sure. Haven't seen her all day. You can check her office."

Half-way up the stairs to the office, a thought came crashing in on Virgil like a thundering herd of wild stallions through a broken fence. He stopped where he could just barely see over the top step and down the hall past the projection room to Marcia's closed office door—which meant that she was probably gone for the day—but another vision appeared in his head. Perhaps there was reason not to alert Marcia of the snafu with Preston Gage. Virgil turned and quickly descended the stairs. Kevin was still on the ladder, carefully applying gold paint to a corner molding with artistic precision.

"Kevin," Virgil said in a complimentary tone. "You certainly are making this lobby a work of art." He gazed around to fully take in the lavish appearance of the room that he had somehow previously overlooked. He seldom came through the front entrance, and lately his focus had been on transforming twenty-first century amateur actors into sixteenth century Shakespearean players; he hadn't noticed Kevin's artisan treatment to the theater lobby.

"Thank you, Mr. Thurston," Kevin replied. "I want it to look as good as the original Crystal Palace did... wanna please Simon... y' know."

"Well, you certainly won't hear any complaints from

Simon, I'm quite sure, or anyone else, for that matter. I, for one, am very impressed." Then Virgil abruptly realigned his focus on Kevin. "I don't know if you are aware," he began, "that Preston Gage has seemed to have lost interest in the theater and in the performance."

Kevin laid his paint brush down on the top step of the ladder, took the towel dangling from his hip pocket and wiped his brow. With a scandalous sort of grin he said, "Well, I suspected something to that affect last night when he threw his script at you and stomped out the back door."

"Yes... well... I intended to apologize for my irrational behavior last night, but he won't answer or return my calls; I've even spoken with his mother, and she can't seem to get any results either. So, I was wondering if you could help me out."

"What? You want me to talk to Preston? What makes you think he'll listen to me?"

"No, no, no. I don't want you to talk to Preston. I think that damage is irreversible. Apologies aren't going to bring him back."

"If you're thinking I can take his place in the play... well... Mr. Thurston, I'm no actor."

"No, no, no. I don't expect that, either."

"What then?"

"Your friend... the one who was sitting with you last night during the rehearsal."

"Jerry Stevens?" Kevin said. "My new groundskeeper? He's a nice guy, but he's a little messed up right now."

"Messed up? What do you mean?" Virgil asked.

"He's dealing with some personal issues."

"Well, he seems to know Shakespeare. He recited Preston's lines quite accurately."

"Oh! So, you want *Jerry* to replace Preston. Is that it?"

Virgil's expression was that of concern. "It's only a week until opening night. I can't possibly expect someone new to learn the part in that short time, unless it's someone who already knows the lines… and your *Jerry Stevens* seems to know them."

"He did mention once that he had belonged to a drama club at Northwestern… said he was an understudy for the play you're doing."

Virgil's eyes widened. "Northwestern?"

Kevin nodded.

"He attended Northwestern University?"

Kevin nodded again. "He said he did."

"An old college buddy of mine, John Buford, is an English Literature professor at Northwestern."

"So…" Kevin said. "Do you want me to talk to Jerry, or do you want to ask him yourself?"

"Perhaps you should talk to him first," Virgil replied. "He may have gotten a misleading impression last night."

"Yeah, you were… well… you weren't exactly yourself last night. I'll talk to him today, and if he's interested, I'll bring him around tonight at six."

12

Keith had remained quite occupied creating the blueprints for Abbey's new restaurant building to be located in Silver Spring; no doubt he would be the first customer. In fact, Robin and Grant, too, were anxious for the café to be functional—and close—so they were all doing everything possible to expedite the project. But none of them were too busy to take notice of changes materializing in their new little town's environment. Not so strange were the many clearly visible cosmetic improvements orchestrated by the new groundskeeper, Jerry Stevens; not that Kevin had done a less effective job of it, but this spring most of his time had been devoted to making the Crystal Palace Theater as magnificent as its name implied. During the off season, the bare shell of a structure that had housed the theater with minimal features other than a stage, lighting, and patron seating had received a complete interior make-over by skilled craftsmen. Until now, it had been not much more than a place protected from the outside elements. But now it truly lived up to its grand name, and the theater-going public was in for a pleasant surprise.

As with any remodeling project, cleaning evolved into the next major undertaking; now that that was complete, Kevin focused entirely on the finishing touches: the mounting of ornately-framed fabulous artwork on the lobby walls, and of course, applying the luxurious metallic gold paint on all the woodwork. That alone had been a monumental task; it was nearing completion, and just in time for the first performance of the new season. The Night Riders were a favorite local band that performed a wide variety of popular music—mostly oldies of '60s, '70s and '80s, Country Rock, and they even put their own spin on a few Swing tunes from the Big Band era. Lately they had graduated from performing in bars to the larger venues, and they even had a record deal pending in Nashville. The locals loved them, and they were sure to fill the house to standing room only come Saturday night.

Along with the completion of the theater, the grand opening of the new hotel—appropriately named the North Star, as it was located near the site of the original North Star Hotel—was close at hand. More and more cars were remaining in the surrounding parking lot overnight, which meant that staff was working around the clock in preparation to accommodate its first guests with reservations, right on schedule, next Friday.

Jeffery Middleton, the new North Star Hotel manager, didn't give much thought or concern to remarks by the construction and maintenance workers who spoke of a stranger sometimes suddenly appearing among them. He would gaze around the new building as if admiring the surroundings, and then he would wander away and disappear around a corner. He was a young fellow, pleasant enough although he never spoke that anyone could recall, but he smiled a lot, and never caused any trouble. His attire seemed out of place—like he had just stepped out of a 1920s movie, but the trend in clothing, lately was difficult to determine if the wearer was making a fashion statement or just didn't know any better. It wasn't until he had been seen on numerous occasions casually strolling through the hotel that the work crews began to realize the stranger wasn't a part of their organization. But with so many theater club members dressed in period costumes wandering around the town, there seemed little reason to be alarmed with this young gentleman.

Jeffery Middleton saw him only a couple of times after the majority of the construction crews had finished their work and were gone, but there was always someone or something demanding his attention; he never had the opportunity to confront the young stranger to ask why he was making such frequent visits to a hotel not yet open for business. When he finally did get a chance to mention the occurrences to Keith, Keith's reply was, "It might be our new groundskeeper... or it could be one of the actors in the drama club; there's always at least two or three of them roaming around in costume."

The answer seemed logical to Jeffery, and their conversation quickly returned to the business of the hotel's grand opening and a brief tour. The old Western décor impressed Keith with its log cabin ambiance. Every inch of the interior—the lobby, the lounge, the restaurant dining room—called out a reminiscing of Old Silver Spring with elegance and charm. The new North Star Hotel was certainly a compliment to the town, and it would surely attract its share of vacationing travelers.

13

At four o'clock on Friday, Kevin was satisfied with his final inspection of the Crystal Palace. Marcia, the theater manager, seemed quite pleased, too, as they meandered through.

"All the paint should be dry enough for tomorrow night," Kevin assured her.

"The sound and lighting crew for the Night Riders will be here tomorrow morning to set up their equipment," Marcia reminded him.

"Yes, I'll make sure Virgil's group has all of their set out of the way."

Without a doubt, the theater was ready for the new season; the interior adornment was finished, and Marcia had everything else under control. Now Kevin had but one thing on his mind; finding Jerry and convincing him to fill in for the missing actor meant keeping the show opening on schedule. Without him, perhaps, the play would not open at all, and that could give the Crystal Palace a black eye right at the beginning of the season.

A quick scan of Main Street rendered no sign of Jerry, but Kevin could hear the faint drone of their riding lawn mower; it seemed to be coming from the picnic area on the east side of the hilltop. Robin, Grant, and Keith had decided the previous year to create a "city park" overlooking the valley and Silver Creek three hundred feet below. The most logical spot was at the end of Flatrock Street; there were a few trees there to provide some shade, and the view was spectacular. It was also a place of significance to the boys, for this was where they first discovered the entrance of the mineshaft that had held their treasure for safekeeping for over a century. The mineshaft opening, on the face of the cliff below the park, was still quite obscure from public view, and the boys made certain that it remained that way with fencing that kept curious hikers away from the land-slide area. Perhaps someday they would make the mineshaft a tourist attraction, but for now, it was their se-cret.

Jerry was only half done with mowing the grassy half-acre. Kevin waved and motioned for him to come to a bench in the shade of a birch tree cluster at the head of the cliff. Jerry drove the machine to the bench and switched off the motor. He had a worried look on his face as he sat down beside Kevin.

"Just wanted to talk to you before you quit for the day and disappeared," Kevin said.

Jerry still didn't lose his concerned expression. "Is my work satisfactory?"

"Yes... everything's great," Kevin assured. "How do you like it so far? You getting along okay?"

"Yeah, I'm really enjoying this. Why do you ask? Is something wrong?"

"No... everything's fine... I just worry that you'll feel like you're missing out on the rest of the world out here."

"What's to miss?" Jerry asked with a grin.

"Restaurants, movies, night clubs… you know… the sort of life that young guys like us tend to enjoy."

"Kevin. Everything I want is right here."

"But this must be a big detour in your life."

"Maybe," Jerry said. "But I'm happy, and a truly happy person is one who can enjoy the scenery on a detour."

"What about your family? Don't you miss them?"

"Sure, I do. But they probably don't miss me, so…"

Kevin threw him a curious stare.

"I've learned," Jerry said, "that people will forget what you said; people will forget what you did; but people will never forget how you made them feel. I caused my family a lot of emotional pain, and it's better if I just stay away." He stared Kevin in the eyes. "Is this what you came all the way out here to talk about?"

"Well, no, actually… didn't mean to pry into your personal affairs… what I did want to talk to you about is the theater."

"Need some last minute help in there?"

"Oh, no," Kevin replied. "The theater is ready. It's the play that's s'posed to open next weekend that needs help."

"Huh?"

"You see," Kevin started to explain. "They lost one of their actors—Preston Gage—and Mr. Thurston noticed that you seem to know those lines. He asked me about it this morning… wondered if you'd be interested in joining them."

Jerry leaned forward, resting his elbows on his knees. "I don't know," he said. "There's not much time left to rehearse—"

"There's as much time for you as there would be for anyone else, except you have an advantage: *you know the lines.* I don't mean to twist your arm, but Virgil's kinda desperate. Preston isn't coming back, and without someone to play the part, the show won't open and that could be detrimental to the Crystal Palace… and to Silver Spring… and to *all* of us."

Jerry sat silent. He thought about the hard work he had put into the theater club back in college, and the disappointment he suffered—although he kept it bottled up, out of sight—when he never was given the opportunity to perform.

"The theater," Kevin continued, "is the lifeblood of Silver Spring; it's the only thing, right now, that generates operating capital, and that makes it a pretty important part of the town."

"But… what if I fail miserably?" Jerry said. "What if I blow it?"

Kevin laid his hand on Jerry's shoulder. "I've known you only a short time, but right now I have more confidence in you than any other player in the cast. If anyone can do this… *you can.*"

For a few long moments, Jerry leaned against the bench backrest and gazed into the treetops. He listened to the breeze shuffling through the leaves and birds singing cheerfully; he filled his lungs with the fresh, clean air and felt the pleasant warmth of the day. For the first time ever, he sensed peacefulness within himself that he had never known before. In the few days he had spent in Silver Spring, he had learned to love the place, and he hated the thought of doing anything that would force him to leave. His failure on the Crystal Palace stage could do just that. But then he thought about the friendship and acceptance he had experienced here like no other place he had ever been. Perhaps, he thought, this was a second chance to live again, to regain control of his existence without being on the run. Yes, this was the place where he could face his past—whatever it may have been—and continue on with his life.

"I... I... I suppose I can give it a try," he said meekly, and then with a firm grip on Kevin's wrist to help accent a changed, stern voice he announced, "But I'm not making any promises."

Kevin breathed a sigh of gratefulness. "A single sincere effort will go a lot farther than a *dozen* uncertain promises. You'll be great. Now... let's go to Wellington for supper; I'll buy. And then we have to get you to the theater. I told Virgil I'd deliver you there by six o'clock."

14

Construction on the new restaurant building would begin soon. Keith had wasted no time to get in touch with his usual contractors, and they assured him there would be crews there within a week. The modular construction method proceeded rapidly; once the foundation was in place, the outside shell of the structure would be up in a few days. If all went smoothly, Abbey's Café would be functional in a month.

Following the brief Saturday morning meeting, Keith remained in the Tanglewood Saloon after the others had left. He sat there thinking about the new project, hoping there was nothing he had missed. Three cats had found their way down the stairs, but soon after their arrival, Rocky and Zeus retreated up the stairs again; only Munchkin stayed, seemingly curious, wandering about. Then, as if he were playing with an invisible toy, Munchkin batted his paws at the air, spinning, rolling and tumbling, thoroughly fascinated with something Keith could not see from across the room. Munchkin wasn't an old cat; he still had plenty of youthful playfulness in him, and he was certainly exercising his kitten functions without the slightest concern of being watched. Keith had seen similar activities of this cat many times before, yet, it seemed like odd behavior, even for a cat.

"Hey, Munchkin! Have you totally gone berserk?"

The verbal taunting didn't even merit the slightest adjustment of those feline ears. Munchkin kept at his game. But in a short while, he came to rest, sitting on his haunches, staring off in the distance, tail twitching occasionally.

Then Keith thought he heard footsteps, but he couldn't determine where they were coming from. Then there was the sound of a closing door. He spun around to see who had entered, but no one was there.

Munchkin trotted to the door, sniffing the air, and then the cat stared forlornly at Keith as if his favorite toy had fallen down a well.

The hair on Keith's arms bristled; he felt a tingling sensation at the back of his neck. Something strange had just happened in that room, but it was as if it had been a dream, untouchable, without substance, a little scary, but fascinating.

Keith wasn't the only one who had a curious encounter that morning. Tanya, Robin's fiancé, had returned to Tanglewood from an early morning trip to the Wellington *Hy-Vee* for a few needed groceries. As she and Robin sat eating a brunch, she was suddenly reminded to ask Robin: "Who was that boy I saw on the stairs this morning?"

"What boy? When?" Robin returned curiously.

"This morning... when I came back from the grocery store. He said he was looking for someone."

"I didn't see anyone," Robin said. "No one came here while you were gone."

"Well, he came down the stairs right past me and went

out."

"What did he look like? Was it the new groundskeeper, Jerry?"

"No, it wasn't him. This boy seemed younger... tall, slender, blond hair... and he was dressed like the actors that roam around Silver Spring."

"Did he say who he was looking for?" Robin asked.

"I think he said *Clancy*, but I can't be sure."

A few moments passed while Robin processed the thought. He knew no one named Clancy, and a tall, slender, blond-haired boy could fit the description of many.

Then he remembered. Clancy. The author of the journal that had led him and his best friends to the treasure at Silver Spring eight years ago. No one else in modern day except Robin, Grant, Keith and Kevin knew about Clancy Crane. Who could possibly be looking for him? It seemed absurd to think that the spirit of one of Clancy's friends from the 1890s had appeared as a real, personified being. Or, maybe it wasn't so absurd; Tanglewood—and all of Silver Spring—had its haunting reputation, and the ghosts of Old Silver Spring had been making their presence known all along. Everyone who lived at Tanglewood had heard the unidentifiable voices; they had all heard the piano music.

"I don't know who that was," Robin told Tanya. "I don't want to cause you alarm..." He hesitated.

Tanya stared at him mildly. "What would there be to cause me alarm?"

"I think you may have encountered our resident ghost."

Tanya laughed. "You're teasing me, right?"

"No... the only Clancy I know lived here in Silver Spring when it was a mining town... in the 1890s. He's the one who wrote the journal that I've told you about. Who would be looking for him is beyond me right now, but I'll find that old journal and try to figure it out."

Tanya's expression changed abruptly from mildly entertained to seriously dumbfounded. "You really think that boy I saw was a ghost?"

"Yes, I do."

"I should've invited him in for brunch."

The early Saturday morning play rehearsal was vitally important now, to give Jerry as much time as possible to work with the rest of the cast. It couldn't be cancelled. Kevin volunteered to be on hand at the theater to make sure everything was out of the way for the Night Riders stage crew to set up for the weekend shows. He sat in the back of the theater watching the actors practicing on stage; they seemed to have progressed with astounding improvement over the last rehearsal he had seen, and Jerry was getting along quite nicely, too, without a script, only needing a bit of occasional prompting. Virgil Thurston seemed extremely pleased with his performance, considering this was only his second time rehearsing with the rest of the cast members.

At a break between scenes when there was a bit of confused scurrying and shuffling about on stage, a man sat down beside Kevin. He was dressed as if he belonged on the stage: black silk top hat, brown, three-piece suit with wide-lapels, and a heavy gold watch chain draped from button to pocket. Tapping his walking stick on the seat in front, he said to Kevin, "If you're worried about your friend, don't. He'll be extraordinary."

Kevin nodded in agreement. "Yeah, I think so too."

"He's a fine young gentleman," the stranger said.

"Yeah, he's a pretty good guy," Kevin returned.

"And that's a magnificent job you have done with the entrance foyer... very flattering."

"Thank you."

Then the man stood, tipped his hat. "Well, I must be off," he said as he pulled out his pocket watch, studied it briefly, and then strutted away toward the doors to the lobby.

Kevin had never seen the man before, and even though he had seemed a bit odd, Kevin was grateful for the compliment he had made regarding the theater lobby. He wondered, though, how the man knew about Jerry.

When the rehearsal was over and all the actors were pitching in to move the sets to the back of the stage where they would be out of the way, he asked Virgil about the man wearing the vintage suit and hat.

"I don't know," Virgil replied. "Doesn't sound like anyone in our group."

15

Sunday morning was strangely chilly. As daybreak claimed its large entrance, birds began chattering their early morning greetings; a rising breeze whispered secrets in the fluttering birch leaves; a chain rattled against the flagpole at the edge of the parking lot. Down in the valley, the creek slowly started taking shape, then color.

Keith had always been a natural early riser, and Kevin hadn't yet adjusted from a regimen of early morning college classes. They both relished the ceremonious sunrise, the unveiling of the new day as they walked together surveying the not yet awake Silver Spring; it was like the King and his favorite knight, both in disguise, who have sneaked out of the castle to visit the peasants' festival. Nothing could hurry them along.

"Good show last night," Keith said, referring to the previous night's concert at the Crystal Palace.

"Yeah," Kevin replied. "Good crowd… and well-behaved." He observed the large parking lot adjacent to the new hotel. "They didn't even leave any litter behind."

It *had* been a very successful opener for the new season—over $8000 in ticket sales, and all afternoon before the show, all the stores and shops had done land office business, too. The Sunday evening show was apt to be less crowded, but there would still be a lot of people in Silver Spring by late afternoon.

As they stood gazing out upon the valley beyond the smelter ruins, the morning sun was just making its grand entrance over the hills. The dew-laden valley grass sparkled like a jeweled cloak and the crisp, cool air carried the smell of pine and wildflowers.

"Don't know if you're aware," Keith said. "There's been some pretty strange things going on around here lately."

Kevin didn't say anything; he just looked at Keith and waited for further explanation.

"Jeffery Middleton, the hotel manager, was telling me the other day that a strange boy has been wandering through the hotel."

"Strange?" Kevin said. "What? Three eyes and purple hair?"

"No, not strange like that. Strange because nobody in the work crew recognizes him, and he's always dressed in old-fashioned clothes."

"Could be someone from the theater group."

"Could be," Keith said. "But he's showed up on days when none of them are here."

"Jerry?" Kevin suggested. "He's been quite interested in everything here."

"Maybe, but that doesn't account for the clothes."

Kevin pondered. He couldn't remember seeing Jerry dressed in anything but shorts and T-shirts.

"Yesterday morning," Keith went on, "Tanya saw a boy on the back stairs at Tanglewood."

"Same one?" Kevin asked.

"Don't know. She said this boy was tall and slim... blond hair."

"Doesn't sound like Jerry."

"He told her that he was looking for *Clancy*."

"Who's Clancy?"

"Kevin... have you forgotten? Clancy's the guy who wrote the journal..."

"Oh, yeah!" Kevin's eyes narrowed to just slits. "What are you saying, Keith?"

"Just wait—there's more. I was sitting in the saloon yesterday morning after our meeting... just relaxing. All three cats came down the front stairs, but Rocky and Zeus couldn't get back up the stairway fast enough."

"Rocky and Zeus don't usually like that room."

"But this was different; it was like something scared them. And then I saw Munchkin playing all by himself, but it didn't look like he was playing alone..."

Kevin frowned. "That doesn't make any sense."

"I know it doesn't," Keith replied. "It's hard to explain. Anyway, a little while later, I heard footsteps and the door closing... but Kevin... there was no one else in the room."

Kevin remained silent, staring off into the distance.

"I know this sounds crazy to you—"

"No, it doesn't," Kevin said. "All this kinda fits in with the man in the theater yesterday morning."

Now it was Keith's turn to be curious. "What man?"

"I was sitting in the back row waiting for the rehearsal

to end… so we could move the stage sets out of the way… and this man who I've never seen before sat down beside me. He told me not to worry about Jerry, and that he liked the job I had done on the theater lobby, and then he just left."

"What'd he look like?"

"Middle-aged, small mustache… suit and vest… and a top hat. A tall, black top hat—one like you'd see in the old movies."

"And he wasn't one of Thurston's people?"

"No. I asked Virgil… said he didn't know who I was talking about."

"Who do you think it might've been?" Keith asked.

"I haven't a clue… unless…"

They both spoke the name simultaneously, "Simon?"

16

To almost anyone else, experiencing the realism of a prior century would seem outrageously far-fetched. When they acquired Tanglewood Lodge and its surrounding territory, Keith Bradley, Grant Kraemer, and Robin Gladstone knew they were moving into an environment where they might be exposed to situations that some might consider frightening. Yet, they felt confident that they could cope with the idea of spirits sharing their space. They invested their time, energy, and money to make this place their home, and to recreate the town as they were able to imagine it.

As youngsters they had set aside any fear of legends that had been handed down through the ages. Their esoteric knowledge of *old* Silver Spring gained from the handwritten journals found in an attic had instilled their courage and strength and determination. Extended exposure to the place proved to them that there was nothing to fear. Their reward for the daring adventure was finding the treasure that no one else knew of its existence, and that treasure, of course, afforded them the opportunity to own the place they had learned to love. Their passion for this forgotten historic place had prompted its incarnation.

Now that the little village was maturing into its former self in appearance, the boys were only vaguely aware of the side affects their efforts had produced. Replicas of old Silver Spring structures had created a wonderful tourist attraction and a novel shopping and entertainment community for the locals, and now it seemed that they had also created a new home front for the spirits of the town's former residents. They probably had a lot of good life experiences in Silver Spring, so it made sense that they would return here. At a time when actors roamed the streets of the newly recreated town, portraying the characters of past times, those spirits could roam, too, unnoticed, and it would be nearly impossible to identify the Real McCoy among the imposters.

But it would soon become apparent that safeguards were necessary, as the public could easily be spooked by rumors of *ghosts* making regular visits; not *everyone* would be so comfortable with the concept.

At the Monday morning meeting in the saloon, Keith told his business partners about Kevin's experience in the theater on Saturday, and they discussed Tanya's episode with the boy on the back stairs and the boy spotted wandering through the new hotel. There was no conclusive answer to any of the incidents.

"It's a good thing," Grant said, "that it was Tanya who saw that boy on the stairs and not Christy. She would've come unglued."

"Is it possible," Robin said, "that ghosts are actually appearing as real people? Now we have *three* incidents where there has been contact with unidentified people."

"Isn't it also possible," said Keith, "that we have some pranksters in our midst? Or maybe some people who are just trying to get in on the act?"

"I suppose that could be true," Robin replied. "But how do you account for the boy telling Tanya he was looking for *Clancy?* No one but us knows about Clancy."

That was a legitimate argument. The boys had been extremely protective of Clancy's journal; anyone else who had ever known about it was long ago deceased, except for Milton Sinclair who had almost ruined their success in finding the lost treasure. But he had left the country, and as far as they knew, he was still spending his inconsequential share of the fortune in South America. He hadn't been heard from since. Clancy Crane had never been a prominent historical figure, so there seemed little chance that his name would hold any significance to anyone now.

"So, what should we do about all this?" Grant asked.

"I don't think we *need* to do anything," Robin replied. "I don't think there's anything we *can* do. If these people are frauds, then they'll eventually be exposed."

"And what if they're not?" Grant argued.

"Then I guess Silver Spring has put a unique twist on the term *ghost town.*"

Not much more could be said about the strange occurrences, but there were other things to discuss.

"How'd we do with the weekend shows?" Keith asked.

Robin referred to his notebook. "After we pay the band, we cleared a little over ten grand."

"Not bad for the first show of the season."

"And the advance ticket sales for next weekend have been phenomenal," Robin added. "Marcia told me that Virgil has agreed to run the play a few more nights. She's getting more tickets printed, and she's contacting the radio stations and all the area newspapers for some more ads."

"Did you know that our new groundskeeper is playing one of the lead roles?" Keith asked.

"No," Robin said. "How did that happen?"

"Kevin told me about it yesterday. One of the actors quit. Virgil was ready to throw in the towel. But then he gave Jerry a shot at the part, and he's been rehearsing with them since Friday."

"How can anyone learn Shakespeare in such a short time?"

"He had some experience with that same play in college."

"Well, then, I guess we owe Jerry a debt of gratitude."

17

Although Kevin had known Jerry only a short time, they had spent enough time together to allow them to become trusting and close friends. Kevin knew there was probably no reason to worry, but he still found himself concerned about Jerry's situation; Jerry didn't really have a place to call home—just a tent somewhere in the woods, and often at night, Kevin wondered if he was dry and warm, and if he had enough to eat. But Jerry seemed so content, like there was nothing unconventional about the nomadic way he was living. It certainly didn't have any effect on his work habits, and it seemed as though he handled the added play rehearsal schedule like it had always been a part of his regular daily routine. Jerry definitely enjoyed a certain sovereignty, but Kevin thought the price of his freedom—total exile from family and friends—seemed more than he could ever possibly pay.

Jerry Stevens was a modern-day Tom Thumb. To some, he was nothing more than a rustle in the dry leaves, a blur of tanned legs and mussed hair. He was driven by a force with features of a child, warlock cunning, strength of a giant, and an animal's endurance. Possessed by that irrepressible male freedom, he seemed to need no one, an independent entity sustained by knowledge and the ability to apply it effectively.

But there was also that inner demon, that intangible ogre that had masked—or perhaps destroyed—part of his memory, and according to Jerry, changed his character and ultimately severed his family connection. Kevin couldn't imagine Jerry any other way; he was a likeable and pleasant person now, and how that personality alteration could be a detriment to family ties escaped him. Apparently, the whole big picture wasn't entirely in focus; there had to be more to that story than Jerry was telling.

Kevin caught up to Jerry as he was sprucing up a flower bed contained within large timbers arranged in a long, rec-tangular shape across the center of the Market Square parking area. The timbers served as a curb where no less than twenty tourists' and shoppers' cars were nosed up to it. The maintenance pickup truck was there, too, with open tailgate facing one end of the garden, its box full of nursery stock and various gardening tools. To Kevin, it almost seemed sacrilegious to disturb Jerry while he performed his artistically magical touch to what, in a couple of weeks, would bloom into a splendidly colorful garden. But Jerry saw him coming and pitched the first greeting. "Mornin' Kevin," he said with a cheerful grin.

"Good morning," Kevin returned.

"When did they deliver the nursery stock?" Jerry asked.

"Saturday afternoon while you were in Wellington at play practice."

"If I'd known," Jerry said, "I could've done this yester-day."

"No, that's okay," Kevin replied. "You need a day off once in a while. And by the way, Robin, Keith, and Grant send their gratitude to you for saving the play."

Hardly noticeable, Jerry's face reddened just a little. "I was glad to do it."

"Are you nervous about opening night?"

"Not yet, but ask me again on Friday afternoon."

"Say, Jerry," Kevin pondered. "Keith told me about some odd things going on around Silver Spring lately."

"Like what?"

"Well, for starters, there's been a stranger that none of the work crews or staff recognizes wandering around in the new hotel. Keith was thinking it might be you."

"I peeked in the front entrance once, but I've never *wandered* through it... wasn't even inside the door."

"Have you seen anyone wandering around who looks out of place?"

Jerry thought a long moment. "There was this cowboy-looking guy..." He pointed to the northwest corner of the Square. "Right over there. But he wasn't wandering... just standing there, mostly."

Kevin looked to where Jerry was pointing. "Hmmm... I'll have to check the map that my brother made... but I think that's where the livery stable stood."

"And then there was that young fella," Jerry added. "Tall, skinny, blond-haired kid... maybe sixteen or seventeen. Had a big yellow dog with him."

"Where? When?"

"That was Saturday morning. He was walking right down the middle of Main Street."

"Did you talk to either of them?"

"No," Jerry said. "Just saw 'em. And the kid with the dog... I've seen him several times. Thought he was someone who lived around here."

"Could be," Kevin said. "It was Saturday morning when Tanya saw that kid on the back stairs at Tanglewood. I wonder if it's the same one."

Jerry just shrugged his shoulders. "Don't know. I'll ask him his name next time I see him."

"So, do you have rehearsal tonight?"

"Yeah... six o'clock. And tomorrow night we start full dress rehearsals... with make-up and the whole works."

"Do you want to go to Abbey's to eat... say, about four o'clock?" Kevin asked.

"Sure."

"Okay. Meet me at the garage at four."

Kevin left Jerry to his gardening and went directly to the new North Star Hotel. So far, there was only one distinct description of the stranger that was sighted by at least two people at different times and places. The tall, slender, blond-haired boy that Tanya met on the back stairway seemed to match the young fellow that Jerry had seen on Main Street. Perhaps Jeffery Middleton might be able to shed some new light on the wandering stranger dilemma.

"I'd like to talk to Mr. Middleton," Kevin said to the gentleman at the front desk.

The desk clerk pointed across the lobby to a small gathering of people. "That's him... the one in the blue—"

"Thank you," Kevin interrupted. He ambled toward the group. Their discussion didn't appear to be official business so Kevin didn't feel that he was intruding. He had spoken with Jeffery many times, so there was no need for introductions.

"Good morning, Kevin," Jeffery greeted.

Kevin acknowledged and offered a handshake. "Good morning. I don't mean to bother you, Jeffery, but could we talk? It won't take long... I know you're busy."

"It's not a bother," Middleton said as he guided Kevin away from the cluster. "What would you like to talk about?"

Kevin scanned the surroundings. The interior of the

North Star was quite impressive with its log walls and Early American décor. "I was wondering if you could fill me in a little more on that stranger you mentioned to Keith."

At first, Jeffery Middleton appeared confused with Kevin's inquiry. "Stranger?"

"Yes, the boy you told Keith you saw—and some of the workmen had seen—but no one recognized."

"Oh! That stranger," Jeffery said. "Well, I don't know anything about him. Is there a problem?"

"No, not yet," Kevin replied. "Did you and the others all see the same boy?"

"Yes, I'm quite sure we all saw the same boy."

"What did he look like?"

Jeffery pondered a moment, trying to get a good mental picture of the stranger.

"Was he tall, skinny, and blond hair?" Kevin suggested.

"Oh, no," Jeffery said. "He was sort of average height and build, and he had dark brown hair... not too long."

"How was he dressed?"

"Dark brown trousers and a pale blue shirt... and suspenders... kinda old fashioned, if you know what I mean."

"Sure, I know what you mean, Jeffery. That's what this whole town is all about... old fashioned."

"Why all the interest in that boy?" Jeffery asked. "Who is he?"

"I don't know," Kevin replied. "But I intend to find out. Is there anything else you can tell me about him?"

"No. Not right now. But if I think of something, I'll get in touch with you."

"Thank you, Jeffery." Kevin offered another handshake. "I think your hotel is absolutely wonderful... and did you get the theater tickets?"

"Yes," Jeffery said appreciatively. "Marcia brought them over last week. We're going to offer them as hospitality gifts to our guests when they begin arriving on Friday."

"That's great! Well, I have to get back to work now. Will we see *you* at the Crystal Palace?"

"I'm not too keen on Shakespeare, but I might give it a go."

Kevin didn't get the answers from Jeffery Middleton that he was expecting. But there had been no vagueness in the description of the hotel wanderer; it hadn't been Jerry. Now there seemed to be *two* mysterious strangers roaming the streets of Silver Spring that weren't necessarily tourists or members of the theater group: one blond-haired boy, and one with dark brown hair. It was a fair assumption that they were just curious local residents. They hadn't caused any trouble yet, and so far, no harm had come to anyone or anything by their presence. But was this the beginning of a potential problem?

I t was merely days, now, until Silver Spring moved into a new era; the new hotel would open for business, offering visitors not only rooms for overnight and extended stays, but restaurant and bar accessible to anyone on just brief sightseeing or shopping visits. Jeffery Middleton, the general manager, was confident that his facility and its staff were ready to meet the expectations of guests with a high level of professionalism. With a large-scale advertising campaign initiated six weeks earlier came a flood of room reservations during the week of the grand opening, promising Silver Spring the start of a busy summer.

The Crystal Palace Theater would welcome sell-out crowds for the presentations of *A Midsummer Night's Dream*, now scheduled to run four additional nights. Marcia had all the necessary elements in place: light, sound and stage personnel to make sure the presentations locked and sounded their best; there were plenty of ushers ready to guide the guests in the right direction, ticket takers at the entrance, and cashiers at the concessions counter and ticket sales window. Ads had been placed with all the local and surrounding newspapers and radio stations; a stellar season was anticipated.

Robin Gladstone, Grant Kraemer, and Keith Bradley weren't just sitting around waiting for things to happen; their little town was growing in leaps and bounds by virtue of their efforts. Four more Main Street store buildings were nearing completion, and construction on Abbey's Restaurant would begin soon. The Wellington County Historical Society was busy at work cleaning up and preserving the old smelter site, preparing it as a tourist attraction, and plans to erect a moderate museum on the original site of the Smith-Hayden Mining headquarters building were being considered.

Silver Spring was getting its second chance as a boomtown, albeit on a smaller scale than had occurred during the Nineteenth Century gold rush. Now, flooding the streets weren't thousands of prospectors seeking gold and silver, but rather, tourists seeking a bit of nostalgia, and perhaps entertainment. In its modern-day variety, visitors weren't forced to navigate muddy thoroughfares, or dodge the hazards of horse-drawn wagons or runaway stagecoaches. Gunfights in the street staged by actors were now less deadly than the original events, and the goods available in the stores were more of the novelty nature than the hard and fast necessities of earlier times.

Kevin considered keeping the information about the unidentified visitors he had gathered to himself, but by mid-afternoon he was anxious to share his findings with Keith, Robin and Grant. Keith, however, was in Wellington meeting with Russell Abbey, and Robin was in a closed door conference with a client.

"Your brother doesn't have anything special going on right now," Judy, their receptionist, informed him.

"Okay... thank you, Judy." Kevin entered Grant's office without knocking. Grant was staring at a computer screen displaying what seemed to Kevin a non-sensible sea of gibberish. It was, however, a complicated, high level program containing some bugs that Grant was attempting to correct.

"Whatcha doin' Bro?" Kevin said. He pulled up a chair and sat beside his brother.

"One of my clients has a severe non-linear waterfowl issue," Grant replied.

"Huh?"

"They don't have all their ducks in a row."

"Oh. Well, why didn't you say that in the first place?"

"What's up, Kevin?"

"Just wanted to tell you what I found out about our mysterious visitors."

Grant dropped his stare at the screen and turned to Kevin. "What have you found out?"

"That we have two strangers prowling around."

"Two?"

"Yeah... the boy Tanya saw on the stairs is not the same one that was seen in the North Star Hotel."

"How do you know they're not the same boy?"

"I talked to Jeffery Middleton this morning... I asked him about the boy in the hotel. He gave me a different description. And Jerry has seen the blond-haired boy several times in the past few days... probably the same one Tanya saw."

"Have you told Robin about this?"

"Not yet... he's in a private meeting. D'ya think there's gonna be a problem?"

"Who knows? But I think it *would* be good to know who they are and what they're doing here. You should talk to Robin."

"Talk to me about what?" Robin poked his head in the open door. "Judy said Kevin was here looking for me." He strolled in, pulled up another chair and sat beside Kevin.

"I talked to Jeffery Middleton this morning," Kevin explained. "He gave me a different description of the boy in the hotel, so there are two boys. And Jerry has seen the blond-haired boy, too."

"Where? When?"

"The last time he saw the boy was Saturday morning... walking down Main Street."

"The same day Tanya saw him," Robin said. "Our ghost boy was busy that day."

"Who do you think it is?" Kevin asked. "Sound like anyone you know?"

"Yeah," Robin replied. "But before I form any conclusions, I want to do some reading."

"That reminds me," Kevin said. "Jerry said he saw another odd man that day, too, just standing around all alone at the northwest corner of Market Square."

"Oh?"

"Jerry said he looked like a cowboy." Kevin turned to Grant. "Where's that map you made from the aerial photos?"

Grant reached for a lower desk drawer, pulled it open and brought out the map, neatly folded and inserted in a nine-by-twelve inch brown envelope. He carefully extracted the map and spread it out on a large table adjacent to his desk.

"Brooke's Livery Stable," Robin said, even before the map was unfolded entirely. He had another copy of the map, and he had committed a good share of it to memory. Because he conducted most of the real estate deals, he knew the layout of the old mining town quite well.

"Maybe it was someone looking for a building lot," Grant said.

"So far, no one has taken much interest in building on

that lot," Robin replied. "Do either of you remember a movie called *Field of Dreams?*"

Keith thought a moment. "Yeah," he responded. "It starred Kevin Costner, I think."

"Right. Do you remember the one line that sort of created the whole theme of that movie?"

Kevin jumped into the conversation. *"Build it and they will come,"* he said. "I loved that movie."

Surprised that the youngster of the group would recall the old movie, it dawned on Grant that the film's storyline involved baseball —sports—his brother's primary interest in life. His career goal was to become a coach.

"What are you suggesting?" Grant asked Robin. "That we build a baseball field?"

"No, not a ball field. A barn."

19

"Hello, John," Virgil Thurston spoke into his cell phone. "How are things at Northwestern these days?"

"Same old rat race," John Buford replied. "And what's worse, I've agreed to teach a summer session. I think I need my head examined."

"Oh, don't be so hard on yourself, John. It'll be over before you know it."

"Sure, and so will the summer. How are things with you?"

"I'm enjoying retirement. You should give it a try."

"Next year, Virgil. Next year for sure. So... how are you occupying your time? Still involved with that community theater?"

"Yes, as a matter of fact. We're opening a new production at the Crystal Palace this Friday."

"Crystal Palace?"

"Yes... the new theater in the old ghost town I told you about."

"Oh, sure... how's that working out?"

"Great, John. They're turning the whole town into a real classy place. And the theater is magnificent. You should see it."

"I'd love to, Virgil, if it weren't so far away. Maybe next summer Laura and I will spend some vacation time there with you. So, what's the production?"

"A Midsummer Night's Dream."

"Shakespeare? In a ghost town? Will there be an audience?"

"It's incredible, John! Three nights sold out with advance sales, so we're running four more performances. Did it do that well at Northwestern?"

"No. But how did you know we did Midsummer Night's Dream."

"Well, that's what I wanted to talk to you about. There's a young gentleman here playing Puck, and he said he was the understudy there at Northwestern a couple of years ago. His name is Jerry Stevens. What can you tell me about him?"

John was silent for a moment while he collected his thoughts. "The name rings a bell... but this is a big school, Virgil, and I see thousands of students. I'm at a loss right at the moment but I'm on my way to the office... only ten minutes away. I'll check his file and call you back."

A half-hour had passed when Virgil's phone rang.

"Yes," John said. "Jerry Stevens. If this is the same one. Sophomore two years ago, twenty years old."

"Sounds right, so far," Virgil replied.

"Biology major... English Lit was an elective, and his scores were extraordinary... a very bright student. And yes, he did participate in our theater group."

"Definitely sounds like the right Jerry Stevens."

"Virgil, I remember this student quite vividly, now that I'm looking at the notes I made. What a sad situation that was."

"What do you mean?"

"He hasn't told you?" John asked.

"He doesn't talk much about his personal life... not to me, anyway. Jerry's been here just a very short time. It was just by chance that I discovered his talent when one of my leads quit with only two weeks before opening night."

"Virgil," John said with a serious tone. "Jerry Stevens dropped out of school several months after he was involved in a bad car wreck. His younger brother was killed, and he couldn't cope with the guilt."

"Guilt?" Virgil said. "What—"

"Jerry was driving the car..."

"Oh. I can see where that might have a significant effect on someone."

"Well, the worst part of the scenario was that he suffered a psychological melt-down. He'd already lost all memory of his brother, and he gradually turned into a person that nobody liked."

"That's hard to imagine, John. The young man is quite likeable now..."

"He finally just quit school and left," John continued. "Mr. and Mrs. Stevens visited me, as they did with several of his professors here, hoping to find clues to where he might have gone. They were devastated, but they admitted that they'd been pretty hard on him about the accident; they blamed themselves for his leaving college... and running away from home."

"He was twenty years old; a legal adult," Virgil added. "You can't exactly call that *running away from home*."

"They told me they had received brief phone calls from Jerry, only to let them know he was okay, but for them *not* to come looking for him."

"Well, I suppose he deserves his privacy... if that's what he wants."

The rest of the hour-long conversation was spent on catching up with their own personal lives. Virgil Thurston and John Buford had been close friends since their college days, but time and distance had diminished their contact. They had plenty to talk about.

Determined to make the Market Square garden plot—and all of Silver Spring, for that matter—a botanical masterpiece, Jerry devoted every ounce of green thumb creativity he had in him. He had sculpted its surface to mounds and valleys with more soil hauled up from the creek banks, added various sized rocks and boulders and even a few weathered wooden posts.

"Why the posts?" Kevin asked.

"For climbing vines," Jerry explained. "There are some flowering Clematis vines in that nursery stock we got last week. It'll be a nice touch."

"How did the dress rehearsal go last night?"

"Okay, I guess," Jerry replied. "You should've stopped in. You could've watched with the three other guys sitting in the back row."

"Who was it?"

"One was the blond-haired boy. The others I hadn't seen before, one young guy, and the other was a little older."

"You're kidding, right?"

"No. They were there."

"Did anyone else see them?"

"I don't know... everyone was too busy fussing with their costumes to notice anything."

"Did you talk to them?"

"No. Didn't get the chance. By the time I was able to get away from the stage, they were gone."

"How about Virgil? Do you think he saw them?"

"Kevin, there are so many people coming and going all the time... I don't think Mr. Thurston pays much attention to someone sitting in the back row."

"What'd the older guy look like?"

"Dark brown suit, I think, neatly trimmed beard... he was pretty far away to see any more."

"Sounds like the guy that sat down beside me last Saturday morning."

"Who are they?" Jerry asked. "Think they're here to cause trouble?"

"I really don't know."

20

A big, glorious blue sky was about the only thing that seemed ordinary in Silver Spring on Friday; it wasn't like any other day. The parking lot around the North Star Hotel began filling with cars—the early arrivals of guests holding reservations. The hotel's indoor swimming pool populated quickly, as did its Silver Pick Saloon adjacent to the main lobby, as did the streets and stores of the village. Adding to the already busy atmosphere, the Parish Construction Company was moving in their equipment to begin the Abbey's Restaurant project. And everywhere there could be felt the excitement and anticipation of the play that would open that night in the Crystal Palace.

As the tourists roamed the village, some casually browsing, and some hustling with purpose, trying to get in as much as possible before they hurried off to their next destination, little did they know that the gardener they passed in the Market Square parking lot, setting an array of Yucca plants in the central garden, was a star of the show. Nor did Jerry pay much attention to any of them, except for one man that watched him working for quite some time. "You're making Silver Spring look really nice," he said after his long stare.

"Well," Jerry replied. "That's what they're payin' me to do." He turned toward the bearded man that seemed vaguely familiar.

"You'll be on stage tonight," the stranger said.

"Yes… we open tonight at eight." Jerry studied the man

without appearing conspicuous. His hat was a bit out of the ordinary, as was his brown suit that looked like it belonged in a museum. It was apparent that the man was one of the roaming actors.

"I've seen some of your rehearsals... very impressive."

"Thank you. Will you be coming to one of the performances?"

"Oh! Indeed! I shall be there tonight. Well, I should not be keeping you from your work. My best wishes to you, and may your performance tonight be extraordinary."

The stranger wandered off and disappeared among the many other people meandering about the streets. Then it occurred to Jerry where he had seen the man before: he was among the three in the back row of the theater during rehearsal a few nights ago. He put down his shovel and went after the man; he wanted to ask his name.

Jerry followed the boardwalk along the short block of Market Street to Main, briefly pausing to catch a quick glimpse in the two small shops. There was no sign of the man in either. To the right on Main, there were only a couple of people near the small bank building that housed an ATM, and there had not been enough time for the man to reach the North Star yet. Dodging pedestrians, Jerry hurried up Main toward the Royal building and the Crystal Palace. Only carpenters and painters were in the two new store buildings on the way, but the Candy Store, the Bakery, and the Gift Shop in the Royal building were almost to the point of being crowded. Jerry threaded his way through each, hoping to spot the elusive stranger. Nothing.

On the next corner was the T-Shirt Shop, equally busy, but it, too, rendered no sign of the man. The front doors of the theater were still locked; up and down the board sidewalks Jerry searched, but the man was nowhere in sight.

Back at the garden plot he resumed the digging and planting, frequently scanning the passing tourists going to and from their cars and the few shops on Market Square. Other than increased pedestrian traffic, nothing seemed out of the ordinary.

When Kevin came by, Jerry was taking a little break, drinking from a water jug.

"You can take the rest of the day off if you want," Kevin said. "I'm sure you don't want to be tired for the play tonight."

"Thanks," Jerry replied. "But I'd rather keep working. I'll just quit a little earlier than usual."

"So... are you getting nervous now?"

"No, but I might if I had too much idle time to think about it."

"Well, then, you can take off whenever you want."

"Okay... and if you want to see at least one of those strangers I told you about, the older one of the three said he'd be at the play tonight."

"You talked to him?" Kevin replied with surprise.

"Just briefly. He watched me here for a while, and then commented on how the garden was looking nice, and by the time I realized who he was, it was too late... he was gone. I tried to find him in the crowd, but I never did see him again."

"Did you get his name?"

"No... like I said, he was gone before I realized who he was."

21

Silver Spring was a very busy place Friday evening. All the parking areas were nearly full; some people had started parking their cars along the roadsides and streets. Ticket holders began filing into the Crystal Palace two hours before the opening performance to insure they would get good seats. Without a doubt, the advance advertising had paid off, and now what the play needed was a good review to hit the morning papers to insure continued standing room only audiences for the remainder of the performances.

Because it was general admission seating, Kevin decided to make sure no one had removed the red ropes that cordoned off the V.I.P. seats in the center front row, reserved for Grant and Christy Kraemer, Robin Gladstone and Tanya, Keith Bradley, and himself. Six additional seats were included to accommodate the Gladstone, Kraemer, and Bradley parents; they had always been fond of live theater shows, sometimes traveling great distances to attend performances. Since the Crystal Palace opened, they hadn't missed a show.

When he saw the red ropes were undisturbed, Kevin headed backstage; one last vote of confidence to Jerry was important. Jerry was still in emotional distress, no matter how calm and collected he appeared. No one knew his background as Kevin did, and a little support would mean a lot. He found the actor leaned back in a chair, half dressed, with a make-up artist fussing about him, trying to create just the right look.

"Hey, Jeanie," Jerry said to the make-up girl. "Here comes the guy who got me into this mess."

Jeanie was an old high school classmate. She turned to Kevin and giggled.

"He had every opportunity to refuse," Kevin said jokingly. "Ready for the big night?"

"As ready as I'll ever be," Jerry replied. "That is... if Jeanie ever finishes with the grease paint."

"Just a few more minutes," Jeanie whined. "You want to look good, don't you?"

Kevin laid a hand on Jerry's shoulder. "Just wanted to wish you well," he said. Then he raised his voice so all could hear: "And to remind everyone in cast and crew that they're invited to the party at Tanglewood after the show."

"We'll be there," came a flurry of responses. It seemed that everyone was in high spirits. It was going to be a great show.

"Are you gonna be watching for you-know-who?" Jerry said.

Jeanie threw them both a puzzled look.

"Just a mutual friend," Kevin explained, and then to Jerry, "I'll be in the front row..."

"Maybe you should be in the back instead," Jerry suggested.

"Yeah, maybe... I guess I could have a front row seat some other night."

Kevin met Virgil Thurston on his way out.

"Will you be attending tonight's show?" Virgil asked.

"Wouldn't miss it," Kevin replied. "After all these years, you've finally gotten me interested in Shakespeare. Will you be coming to the party at Tanglewood after the show? Keith wanted me to remind you."

"I will... that is... if the show doesn't turn out to be an embarrassment."

They both laughed

"Okay," Kevin said. "See you there." He shook Virgil's hand and slipped out the side door. He had plenty of time to shower and get dressed.

Keith didn't have to be curious as to why Kevin was so anxious to get to the theater early. He was quite aware of Kevin's close friendship with Jerry, but arriving a full half-hour before curtain time seemed a little extreme, especially when they had reserved seats. "Why so early?" he asked.

"I'm hoping to see someone there," Kevin replied.

"Who?"

"I'll let you know after I see him." Kevin didn't want to arouse any more curiosity that might create a disturbance in his plan to meet the mysterious stranger. And depending on the results of that meeting, he would decide if it was anything worth sharing.

After seven-thirty the theater filled quickly to capacity; a few people had elected to stand along the rear wall when all the seats appeared to be taken. Kevin casually waved to Keith, Grant and Robin as they and the rest of their party were ushered to the seats in the front row. He had already instructed the usher to inform them that he would join them a little later, perhaps during an intermission. In the meantime, he studied the crowd, looking for the bearded man in the brown suit. It was a pleasantly warm evening, so many of the men had removed their jackets; searching for a brown one might be futile. A beard might be easier to spot.

When the house lights went down just before curtain time, Kevin thought he might be hunting for a melon seed in a pile of sawdust. He saw a few brown jackets and a few beards, but not the ones he was looking for.

The crowd hushed and the curtain parted; the elegant set depicting the luxurious interior of an Eighteenth Century castle parlor emerged from the dark stage. Three actors entered from the wings; customary applause rose from the audience as the actors found their marks. Kevin wasn't paying much attention to what was happening on stage. His gaze focused on a figure along the back wall that he hadn't noticed before. In the dim light it was difficult to tell for sure, but he thought the man fit the right description. Slowly and cautiously he made his way up the side isle to where the man leaned against the wall.

More applause sounded from the audience as four more characters entered the stage.

"Are you enjoying the show... Simon?" Kevin whispered.

The bearded man tilted his head toward Kevin and whispered his response: "My name isn't Simon. I'm Tom."

"I saw you here last Saturday morning, didn't I?"

"You most certainly did."

"Can we talk some more? During the next intermission?"

"That could be arranged."

"Great!"

Tom nodded in acknowledgment.

Kevin smiled and then turned his attention to the stage where the beautiful Hermia was being threatened with her life if she didn't agree to marry the young man her father had arranged for her to wed. Hermia, of course, was in love with another, and was ready to die rather than marry a man she didn't love. Kevin had watched rehearsals enough to know that Jerry wouldn't be on stage until the beginning of Act Two after the first intermission, so he had time to think about what questions he would ask of Tom. But he wasn't about to move from the spot where he stood; he wouldn't give the stranger a single opportunity to disappear without the promised conversation.

All through the first act, the man—Tom—seemed to be paying very close attention to the play. He was awed by the elaborate stage sets, and he was definitely impressed with the theater.

22

Keith, Robin, and Grant headed to the lobby during the first short intermission, while the girls headed to the ladies' powder room. None of them noticed Kevin talking with the stranger in a dim corner at the back of the theater.

"You must really enjoy Silver Spring," Kevin said.

"Oh, yes, indeed! It has once again become such a wonderful place."

"Why are you here so often?" Kevin asked.

"I'm a newspaper reporter. Keeping up with the daily news is what I do," Tom replied.

"Newspaper? Which newspaper?"

"I used to be on the staff at the Wellington Daily News. Now I'm what you would call freelance."

"You submit articles to different papers?"

"You might say that."

"So, are you covering the play tonight? Or are you just here for the pleasure?"

"Both. I'm thoroughly enjoying the performance, and perhaps I will submit a review."

"I hope you'll put in a good word about the theater."

"Oh, you can count on it, my friend."

The house lights dimmed and immediately brightened again to alert the audience that the show would resume momentarily.

"Well, Tom," Kevin said. "I should get back to my seat. The rest of our party is probably wondering where I disappeared to."

Tom nodded his approval.

"Will I see you again this summer?"

"Most assuredly."

Kevin joined Robin and Keith on their way back to the front row seats. Christy, Grant, and Tanya returned just as the lights faded and the curtain parted for the beginning of Act Two.

From what Kevin knew of the play, he expected Jerry—portraying the mischievous elf named Robin Goodfellow but commonly referred to as "Puck"—to be costumed like Peter Pan. But to his pleasant surprise, Puck appeared more like Robin Hood as he entered the stage now resembling a forest. It was all part of Virgil Thurston's interpretation and treatment of the Shakespearean play, giving it more appeal to a modern audience. Not only had he advanced the costumes, but dialogue was slightly altered to make it more understandable, and so far, this audience loved it.

There was no denying that Jerry was delivering a good performance because of audience reactions; every time he came on stage there was applause, and when he applied the nectar from the magical flower to eyes of the wrong sleeping lovers, there were chuckles and giggles. But when he played his mischievous tricks—like changing the head of another character into that of a donkey—there were whistles and cheers and uproar of laughter. Never before had

Shakespeare been so well received by a small town audience.

The stage seemed to swallow him, as if he had been poured from a bottle and transformed into another tangible mass. He knew the story well—the threat of Theseus; the mishap in the forest; the curious flower; the sleep; the arrival of dawn and the Duke's acceptance to the previously disputed love—all transported him to another world where character could readily be calculated, a world where menace foreshadowed catastrophe, where evil was conquered and love exalted. His emotions were contained within durable boundaries because there, everything evolved with the logic of art, not real life.

By the time Jerry conveyed his closing lines—the little speech at the very end of the play that suggested this might have all been a dream, and then asking for the viewers' forgiveness—he had certainly gained a few admirers, and many of the four hundred people had different attitudes toward Shakespeare.

After the five-minute standing ovation for the final bows, Kevin looked to the back of the theater. He hoped to see Tom and gain his attention; he hadn't thought earlier during their brief conversation to invite him to the cast party at Tanglewood. That would certainly be the perfect opportunity for a newspaper man to get the "inside scoop" for his story. But Tom had apparently left.

As Kevin and Keith exited the Crystal Palace, Keith recalled that Kevin had arrived early to meet someone. "Did you see whoever it was you came early to see?" he asked.

"Yes, I did."

"Is it still a secret?"

"No, it's no secret. The guy I saw last Saturday morning? Turns out he's a freelance newspaper reporter."

"Is he coming to the party?"

"I forgot to invite him," Kevin said. "I was hoping to see him again after the play, but it looks like he's already gone."

"We'll probably see the story in the paper tomorrow." Keith stopped outside the front entrance. "I'm going to the North Star with Robin and Grant for a drink... see how their opening is going."

"I'd join you," Kevin responded. "But I'd better make sure the cast doesn't destroy Tanglewood. They're apt to be in pretty high spirits."

"Good idea," Keith said. "We'll be there later."

23

An assembly of dark figures paraded from the theater, converging in the pool of light on the front lawn at Tanglewood. They were, of course, the cast and crew of *Midsummer Night's Dream*, carrying six-packs, coolers, brown paper bags and pizza boxes. When Kevin first saw them in the light he thought that he, himself, was a bit over-dressed for this party, still wearing the sport coat he wore to the theater, as the troupe looked more like a band of hoboes in their backstage attire of faded jeans, tattered sweatshirts, washed out T-shirts, and grubby sneakers—a drastic change from the more flattering onstage garb of less than an hour before. Just as Kevin had anticipated, the whole group—about thirty—were in high spirits following the success of opening night. Lighthearted and jovial laughter accompanied the chattering voices as they filed in past Kevin, welcoming them as they entered. But once inside, the banter subsided; eyes popped and jaws dropped. Hardly any of these people had ever seen the 1890s Tanglewood saloon before that very moment, and most were in awe of this grandly restored Nineteenth Century tavern. Overhead, the massive, honey-colored oak beams reflected the glow from the crystal chandeliers, and the simple yet elegant wooden furniture offered a warm and friendly invitation for a social gathering. The partiers quickly deposited the refreshments and food on the gallant old bar and continued their gawking for a few more minutes. For the first time in history, the members of the Wellington Theater Club were speechless. They wandered about gazing upward at the interlocking beams, and then down at the highly polished hardwood floor with its huge complimentary Persian rug in front of the antique upright piano. Then they collected their wits and all began talking at once.

"Kevin! Do you actually live here?"

"This is *so* neat!"

"I can't believe it... it's like a museum."

"Who did the restoration?"

"Look at the size of those beams."

"Kevin, darling, it's marvelous. Would you consider time share?"

Kevin was well acquainted with many of the group, and he had met the others at one time or another. Some were close friends from his school days at Wellington High.

Richard Landers, local hardware store owner, had auditioned for the part of King Oberon, but director Virgil Thurston thought better of that and cast Richard as Theseus, the noble Duke of Athens.

Amy Landers, president of the theater club, was everyone's friend. Virgil had chosen her to play Hippolyta, the Duke's fiancée; she and Richard made a good couple—on *and* off the stage.

Kari Odell, daughter of the former mayor had wanted

the lesser role Hippolyta, legendary Queen of the Amazons, but she was perfect for the role of Titania, Queen of the fairies.

College student home for the summer, Jared Osborne, Kevin's long-time friend and soccer teammate, was cast as King Oberon; on stage, he and the beautiful Titania were at odds over a young Indian prince that Titania refused to give in to Oberon's wishes to make the boy a knight. Off stage, however, Jared and Kari were good friends.

Meredith Donaldson looked ten years younger than she actually was. A petite, soft spoken bank teller in real life, she could project fury on the stage, just right as Helena, one of the young lovers entangled in Shakespeare's web of jealousy. Meredith had been flirting with Kevin Kraemer ever since he opened his own bank account at the age of seventeen.

Adam Hall and Derek Collins were both a couple of years older than Kevin, but they had all been friends in high school—not particularly close, but friends. Neither Adam nor Derek had entered college, and their interest in the local theater club added some wonderful talent. They played Demetrius and Lysander, the two young men who became victims of mistaken identity, and both fell into the outrageously laughable love affair with the same woman.

Kevin moved about the celebration, offering congratulatory chit-chat whenever appropriate. He wasn't surprised to see Jerry Stevens surrounded by several female members of cast and crew.

Virgil Thurston was there, too, the best dressed individual among the raggle-taggle group in his custom tailored suit and highly polished wingtips. He sat conservatively at the bar sipping his drink. Just as Kevin approached Virgil,

Amy Landers nudged his elbow. "Look at your friend, Jerry over there with his admirers. But I guess if I wasn't happily married to Richard, I'd be there, too."

Kevin gazed across the room to where Jerry seemed to be enjoying the attention he was receiving. "Yes," he replied. "He *is* a very likeable guy."

By then, nearly everyone had once again realized their desire for food and drink, and the bar area was becoming quite crowded as the pizza boxes flew open and multiple hands grabbed at the fare. Corks popped from several champagne bottles and the bubbly dispensed to anyone with a glass.

Munchkin, Rocky, and Zeus had been lured to the edge of the balcony overlooking the soiree by the tantalizing aroma of pizza sausage and pepperoni. But the noisy crowd was more than they cared to engage, so despite the delicious food smells, Rocky and Zeus retreated to the other end of the building. Munchkin, though, stayed and watched. He had some friends among the group, and perhaps someone would notice him there and bring him a slice of pizza.

"Where did you get the pizza?" Kevin asked his friend Jared Osborne. He'd seen Jared carrying in one of the large boxes.

"We called the new hotel before the performance... arranged for them to have it ready. A couple of the stage crew went over and picked them up. You'd better dig in before it's all gone."

Kevin sampled the pizza. Sausage and mushroom. His favorite. Another plus for Silver Spring. The North Star made pizza. *Good* pizza.

While he munched on another slice of pizza, Kevin noticed a fellow beside the upright piano, his gaze scanning the room as if looking for someone. He seemed alone, although he must have been part of the stage crew.

"Who's that guy over by the piano?" Kevin asked Virgil. "I've not seen him before."

Mr. Thurston peered in that direction. "I've seen him around the theater during rehearsals, but I don't know who he is."

"You mean... he's not a member of the stage crew?"

"Not that I am aware," Virgil said.

Kevin contemplated going over to talk with the fellow, but at that moment, Keith, Grant and Christy, Robin and Tanya made their entrance. For the time being, they dominated all the attention with compliments to all the performers, shaking hands with everyone as they mingled among the crowd.

"That was a magnificent performance," Robin told the cast members. "And my hat's off to the people who created those sets. They're fantastic! And to all the crew and anyone else who had a hand in it... I say bravo!"

Grant took his turn to congratulate the troupe. "For the first time in my life," he said, "I can actually understand Shakespeare!"

The room erupted in laughter. "That goes for most of us, too," someone shouted, and the laughter and cheers rose even higher.

"How was the opening at the North Star?" Kevin asked Keith when the noise had settled and everyone was back to normal conversation.

"They were busy," Keith replied. "The bar was full and the dining room had a waiting list. Jeffery told me they had only three vacant rooms."

"It's good that they're off to a good start."

"Yes, but Jeffery mentioned a little disturbance that occurred this afternoon."

"What?" Kevin asked.

"Remember the strange boy that no one recognizes?"

"Yeah…"

"He got into an argument with another guy in the lobby."

"Who was the other guy?"

"Well, Jeffery didn't know… another stranger… and he wasn't a hotel guest."

"What was the argument about?"

"Jeffery didn't know that, either. By the time he could get to them, they had taken the fight outside. He didn't see them again."

"That reminds me," Kevin said. "There's a guy here… I saw him just before you came in… over by the piano." He turned to get another look at the stranger, but he was no longer in the same place he had been. Kevin searched the room, but the young man was nowhere to be seen.

"What'd this guy look like?" Keith asked.

"Average build, brown hair, about twenty, I'd say…"

"Sounds like the same guy Jeffery saw at the hotel."

Jerry nudged Kevin after making a stealth approach. "What did you guys think of the performance?" he said.

"It was outstanding," Keith offered. "How did you learn that part so quickly?"

"Oh, I already knew it… from my college days. I just had to learn Mr. Thurston's variations… that was the hardest part."

"Well, you made it look easy. You were magnificent."

"Thank you, Keith. And what about you, Kevin?"

"You were great, but I'm sorry, Jerry. I still don't get

Shakespeare."

Jerry laid a hand on Kevin's shoulder and gave Keith a sarcastic grin. *"Lord, what fools these mortals be,"* he spoke in his character voice.

"Maybe," Kevin said, "If I see the play about twenty more times I might half understand it." He scanned the room again, hoping to catch a glimpse of the stranger.

"You saw him, too, didn't you?" Jerry said.

Kevin eyed his friend with curiosity. "The guy by the piano earlier?"

"Yeah," Jerry replied. "I'm almost certain that's the guy I saw walking down the street last Saturday."

24

Sunday morning, after two successful performances of *Midsummer Night's Dream*, Keith Bradley was anxious to see the reviews in the Wellington Daily News Sunday edition. As usual, three copies had been delivered to the front veranda of Tanglewood. He picked them up and returned inside, leaving two copies on a table in the saloon where Robin and Grant would easily find them.

The Sunday paper almost always contained news and articles of interest about Silver Spring, "the up and coming new community of magnetic appeal." That line that had appeared in an earlier edition had always amused Keith; for over a hundred years this plot of ground had remained repulsive to the local population simply because of a legend. Now, because of Keith and his two partners, Robin Gladstone and Grant Kraemer, that legend was the very strength that made Silver Spring so appealing, and the locals were flocking in to enjoy the novelty of this new attraction.

Keith was particularly interested in this issue; a couple of events were bound to have attracted attention of the press. The opening of the new hotel would surely warrant at least a half-page spread, and the very popular play at the Crystal Palace would certainly have registered some reviews.

Munchkin joined him as he eased back into the sofa and opened the paper to the "Community" section where usually were the Silver Spring articles. He didn't have to search.

"Lookit here, Munchkin," he said quietly. "There's an

article about the North Star."

"Mraow."

On the first page, a large color photo of the North Star Hotel, nearly full parking lot, and an artistic sunset background occupied the top quarter, and various smaller interior photos and the story filled the rest of the page. It was quite impressive; Keith thought Jeffery Middleton should be rather pleased.

On the next page he found the play reviews—not one, but two. The first one was by Shelly Deering, the journalist whose stories most often appeared on matters of local live entertainment. Her piece on *Midsummer Night's Dream* presented at the Crystal Palace was quite flattering, giving director Virgil Thurston ample kudos for his treatment of the script, set designs, casting, and the performance in general. As an avid fan of classic plays, Shelly seemed quite impressed with the modernized dialogue but the retention of the more correct settings and costumes, admitting that she liked the more believable "elf" portrayal of Jerry Stevens' character, Robin Goodfellow, over the commonly and usually grotesque presentation of Shakespeare's intended "fairy."

Flattering, too, were her critiques on the actors and actresses, particularly Jerry Stevens in one of the lead roles. About him she wrote: *In countless versions of this play that I have viewed, never before has there been a Robin Goodfellow—Puck, that is—played by such a remarkably talented actor; a more perfect match could not have been cast. His performance was flawless, and there can be no doubt that he left a few teary eyes in the audience with his closing recitation, suggesting that this whole ordeal was, perhaps, a dream.*

Then Keith went on to the next article, simply titled COMMAND PERFORMANCE. It had been submitted by Tom Hargrove; this had to be the reporter that Kevin had met at the Friday night show, one of the mysterious visitors to Silver Spring. The name seemed vaguely familiar, but Keith just couldn't place it. But whoever he was, Tom was a prolific wordsmith, giving such flair to his observations as Keith had not read before: *At the regal Crystal Palace Theater on Friday evening, the Shakespearean comedy,* Midsummer Night's Dream *was performed with such eloquence and finesse that has heretofore not been experienced by any audience sitting before that stage. Even the playwright, William Shakespeare himself would have been rendered to tears.*

The journalist went on to rave further about the play, the actors, the elaborate stage sets, the extraordinary lighting and sound effects... and the magnificent theater, *a wonderful reminiscence of the original opera house that once occupied that very spot in Silver Spring. Although it is not an exact duplication, the warmth and beauty of the original radiates from its walls. What a splendid compliment to our community!*

Kevin was still sound asleep, and would be for the next couple of hours. But Keith thought that Robin or Grant might be up by now. He opened the apartment door and glanced down into the saloon where he had left the papers. One was gone, and he guessed that Robin had been there.

Passing quietly through his back door and down the hallway, he stopped at Robin's apartment door; soft radio music came from within, so he knew someone was up. He knocked softly on the door.

"Good morning," the young lawyer said when he saw Keith. "I thought it might be you."

"Morning," Keith replied. "Did you see the paper?"

"Yes," Robin said.

"Some pretty impressive articles, eh?"

"Impressive… and puzzling."

"Puzzling? Why?"

"Did you happen to notice the byline on the second review?"

"Yeah… it's that reporter that Kevin met Friday night."

"Tom Hargrove? Wait here," Robin said. "I'm going to get something from my office. I'll be right back."

When the door closed behind Robin, Keith poured himself a cup of coffee and sat down at the breakfast bar where the Sunday paper was open to the Silver Spring articles. He studied the byline again—Tom Hargrove—but it still didn't register. He thought maybe he had seen that same byline with some other article in the past, and that's why it seemed familiar to him.

Robin came back carrying an old, leather-bound book. That book *was* familiar—it was the old journal that had led Robin, Grant, and Keith to the fantastic treasure in the mine shaft.

"What did you get that for?" Keith asked.

Robin opened the book, paged through it until he came to the passage he wanted to show Keith. He put the journal down in front of Keith and pointed to a line. "All through his journal," Robin said, "Clancy writes about a newspaper man named Tom. In a couple of places, he mentions Tom's surname—Hargrove."

Keith read the lines in Clancy's entry about rescuing his friend who had been abducted by bank robbers as a hostage: *Tom Hargrove wrote in the Striker that it was busting up all those guns that got them caught…*

"I wanted you to see it for yourself," Robin said.

"I remember now," Keith replied. "But it must be just a coincidence."

"Try to find that name in the phone directory," Robin suggested.

Keith eyed he local phone book on the table. "I'd guess that you already have," he said.

"Yes, I have."

"Then, I guess there's no point in me looking."

"Tomorrow morning I'll check with Bill Collins at the Daily News. He'll know who this guy is."

25

E xcavation for the foundation for Abbey's Restaurant building started mid-morning on Monday. There were concerns that the close proximity to the Crystal Palace might create problems during the remainder of the biggest show the theater had presented so far. It had been decided at the Monday morning meeting that Keith should advise the construction crew not to block any walkways or streets, at least until after the play closed.

"Don't worry," Dave Parish told Keith. "We'll keep everything contained behind the sidewalk for now."

"That's good," Keith said. "And then I have another little project I'd like to show you."

"Another project?"

"Yeah... when you can work it in." Keith turned and pointed toward the far corner of the Market Square. "We'd like to put up a barn on the far side of the Square."

"A barn?"

"Yeah. Just a simple pole barn... with this façade facing the street." He unfurled a large sketch revealing his interpretation of the 1890s livery stable that once occupied that lot.

Dave studied the rough draft drawing. "How big is this *barn* gonna be?" Dave asked.

"About forty feet across the front... maybe thirty feet deep."

"Oh," Dave said. "That's just an outhouse compared to the Crystal Palace."

"Yeah... nothin' fancy... just a barn. Water and electricity... and a concrete floor, of course."

"Do you have the building permit?"

"Robin will have it by the time you're ready to start."

As the contractor verbally described the simple structure, it was apparent that he was thinking out loud, mostly, and Keith was paying more attention to a bystander who was closely observing the backhoe digging a deep trench—the beginning of the large hole that would become Abbey's basement. "Is that one of your crew?" he asked Dave.

Dave stared at the young man for a moment. "No, that's not one of my men. I think he's one of your actors... y' know... one of the Silver Spring ghosts."

"It's kinda early for any of them to be here," Keith replied. "He looks as nervous as a jack rabbit in a forest fire."

They continued to discuss the construction of the future barn and the nature of Keith's two-story false front to simulate the 1890s Brook's Livery Stable; it would certainly make the structure appear much larger, but more important, it would be a fitting addition to Market Square.

"All my carpenters are busy building the modules for Abbey's while the concrete work is getting done here," Dave said. "But they could start on it right after."

"No rush," Keith said. "We want Abbey's up and running as soon as possible."

Keith didn't see the curious bystander leave, but when he and Dave had concluded their discussion, the guy was gone. Keith headed back to his office at Tanglewood.

"I've been looking for you," a strange voice said.

Jerry looked up from his work in the Market Square garden. He sucked in a hardly noticeable gasp as he stared at the slovenly attired young man standing before him with solemn expression, perhaps, desperate. "Why were you looking for me?" Jerry asked.

"Because I think I can trust you," the stranger said.

The fellow wasn't exactly a stranger; Jerry had seen him many times, most recently during the cast party at Tanglewood after the opening night performance of *Midsummer Night's Dream*. He was the mysterious stranger who had eluded everyone, and now, for some seemingly odd reason, he was seeking trust.

"And just exactly why do you trust me?"

"Because you're not like the others."

"What d'ya mean?" Jerry asked.

"You're not greedy. You're satisfied to work as a gardener, something you love, when you could be something much bigger and more prosperous, but you don't because you wouldn't love what you do. That's honesty in its purest form."

"For what reason do you need *my* trust?"

"To keep Silver Spring from being destroyed again."

"Whoa!" Jerry exclaimed. "You're getting into some pretty heavy stuff. What makes you think Silver Spring is in danger of being destroyed?"

"I know things," the boy said bluntly. "But we can't talk here. We need some privacy."

Jerry thought a moment. "The only place I know would be my campsite."

"That will do. I'll meet you when you're done working."

"Well, I'd better tell you where it is... it's—"

"I know where it is," the boy interrupted. "But I'll meet you here and we'll go together... about three?"

"Y-Yeah... o-okay," Jerry said. "But I have to be back at the theater by six."

The boy nodded, turned and walked away, mingling into a crowd of people. Somehow, Jerry knew he wouldn't see him again until three o'clock. Until then, though, he had a lot of flowers to plant. He considered informing Kevin about his contact with the mysterious visitor, but that would be dishonoring the boy's trust. Until he learned what the boy had to disclose, there would be no harm in keeping the meeting confidential. On the other hand, if there really was a bona fide threat to Silver Spring, he would feel obligated to pass on the information.

On his routine afternoon trip around the village collecting the trash from the randomly placed receptacles, Kevin stopped the utility tractor and trailer at the end of the Market Square garden plot. Cars filled all the parking spaces on both sides, nearly concealing Jerry's position. He spotted the horticulturist at the far end among a grouping of shrubs. He hadn't seen much of Jerry all weekend, other than at the theater on stage.

"There you are," he said as he approached and watched Jerry distribute wood chips to cover the bare ground around the plants. "It's almost three o'clock. Would you like to get something to eat at the North Star? They shouldn't be too busy right now... I know you have to be at the theater by six."

Jerry looked at his wristwatch. Although the offer was tempting, he said, "Um... no thanks... not today. I just want to go get cleaned up and rest a little while."

"Okay, suit yourself," Kevin said. "Did you happen to see the reviews in the Sunday paper?"

"Um, yes, I did. I saw them yesterday when I was in town." Even though Kevin was his best friend, right then was not a good time for chit-chat. He only had ten minutes to gather his tools and return them to the garage, and he knew if Kevin was there, the mystery boy would probably not appear. "Well," he said. "I have to get my tools put away."

"Put 'em in the trailer," Kevin offered. "I'll take them back to the garage." He sensed that Jerry was putting him off; it didn't seem like Jerry.

"Thanks," Jerry said as he placed the shovel, rake, and several miscellaneous tools in the trailer. "I don't mean to be short, but will I see you at the theater tonight?"

"More than likely," Kevin replied. "Break a leg." He mounted the tractor, started the motor and pulled away.

In the corner of his eye, Jerry detected the boy coming toward him. He turned and started walking. They met at the end of the garden, and without speaking a word, they headed toward the southern perimeter of Silver Spring.

Their leaving together was not unnoticed. Kevin was on his way to the North Star when he caught a glimpse of them just as they neared the trail leading past the smelter ruins and toward the creek. Jerry's campsite was in that direction. There was little doubt that the person walking with Jerry was the curious bystander he had seen earlier that morning at the construction site, who looked suspiciously like the fellow next to the piano at the Friday night party.

26

It seemed almost odd to Jerry arriving at his campsite accompanied by someone else. No one else had ever been there —not even Kevin. This was his place of solace, his sanctuary, his retreat from the rest of the world, where his privacy had not been disturbed. Why he had invited a total stranger to be his first guest puzzled Jerry; he had been quite careful about sharing the exact location of his "home" with anyone. Not that he was worried about pilferage—he didn't have much to steal; a few clothes, tent, sleeping bag, small cooler, and a ten-dollar transistor radio. Any other valuables he always kept with him. It was the seclusion he had been protecting.

"Why do you live out here all by yourself?" the boy asked.

Jerry thought a moment, wondering how much he really wanted to reveal to someone he really didn't know. "In all honesty," he began, "I sort of ran away from my life, and I'm keeping a low profile."

"Why did you run away?"

"Because I didn't like the person I was... and nobody else did, either." Jerry sat down on the ground next to his tent, and then gestured for his guest to do the same.

"I did that once," the boy said as he sat down. "But I did it to see what was at the other end of the river."

"And what did you find?" Jerry asked.

"A big, beautiful world, so full of wonders I can't count them all."

"Oh, I found a big, beautiful world, too. I just wish I could find myself."

"You will, my friend. You will."

"So," Jerry said. "What is it that you needed this privacy to tell me?"

"Oh, yeah, that. How much do you know about Silver Spring?"

"Well, I know that it's owned by some really good people, and—"

"No, no… I mean the *old* Silver Spring… the way it *used* to be."

"You mean about the history?"

"Yeah."

"Only what Kevin told me when I first came here… about how some bank robber killed the owner of Tanglewood and then he set fire to the whole town."

"That was McDowell," the boy responded. "Did he tell you what happened to McDowell?"

Jerry thought a moment. "Yeah… the hotel owner's brother clubbed him… right outside the hotel… killed him. But he never got blamed for it because everyone thought it was the hotel owner's ghost getting revenge. I guess that's how the legend about the place got started."

"Well, that's partly true. Do you think the brother should've been punished for killing the bank robber?"

"No, I don't think so," Jerry replied.

The boy seemed to like Jerry's response. "Why?"

Jerry shrugged his shoulders. "I don't know..."

"I'll tell you why," the boy said. "Because he was doing what he thought was right. The vigilantes where hunting McDowell, and they were gonna kill him anyway... *if* they caught him. And yes, there was probably a strong feeling of revenge involved, too."

"That makes sense," Jerry said. "It seemed justified."

"Did Kevin tell you about Oliver Pratt?"

Jerry shook his head with vagueness in his eyes.

"Oliver Pratt was the guy who stole the silver and gold from the smelter and hid it in the old mine shaft, one bar at a time. It took him months."

Jerry eyed his visitor, now with suspicion. "I s'pose this is all in that book that Robin has locked in the vault."

"Some of it, but not everything," the boy replied.

"Is that the gold and silver that Kevin's brother found?"

"Yes. And without a little help, they might not have found it."

"Help?"

"Yes. Keith used a walking stick to test the bottom of the stream they had to cross in the mine shaft. It fell from its resting place when they were in the cavern where the ingots were hidden... under the water. It startled them, but then Robby got the idea to test the pool of water with the stick, and that's how they found the gold and silver."

"But it doesn't sound like they had any help—"

"The walking stick fell because it had a little push."

"By who?"

"Let's just say they weren't alone in that tunnel."

Jerry had never been told the details of the actual discovery beyond the fact that the treasure was found in the abandoned mine. He didn't even know where the mine was located, and he didn't have any reason, now, to doubt this boy who seemed quite well-informed on the matter. But he was still puzzled. "So, what does all this have to do with Silver Spring being in danger?" he asked.

"I'm getting to that," the boy replied. "Did your friends tell you about their exploration through the rest of the mine?"

"No, they didn't..."

"When Robby, Grant, and Keith finally found the mineshaft, and before they actually found the treasure, they wandered through a lot of the tunnels and caverns left from where the silver was taken out... but they only saw part of it—a *small* part of it. They came to a place where the shaft had caved in and they couldn't get any farther. So they tried other passages, and found nothing but big empty caverns."

"But there must've been more to it than what they saw," Jerry commented.

"You're catching on quick," the boy said. "Beneath the town there is a whole network of tunnels and huge caverns. It's where the majority of the silver was mined, and what made Silver Spring so wealthy. But when the last cave-in happened—the one that closed off the main shaft where Robby and Keith and Grant couldn't go any farther—the mining company decided to close that mine, because they had others farther away from the town that were just as prosperous."

"So, the mining operations didn't stop entirely?" Jerry said.

"No. Mining went on for several years after that... just not in that particular mine. Several cave-ins had claimed the lives of many men, and in the last one, three miners died, and their bodies were never recovered."

"You mean... they never tried to dig them out?"

"It was too dangerous. There was the chance of more tunnels collapsing and more men getting killed. So they just closed the mine."

"But you still haven't told me why Silver Spring is in danger."

The boy looked at Jerry in such a way that Jerry knew he was seeking trust and expecting confidence. "Those big digging machines next to the Crystal Palace..."

"What about them?" Jerry asked.

"They must stop digging!"

"Why?"

"If they re-open that mine, the caverns under the town will cave in. The Crystal Palace and everything on Main Street will be swallowed by the earth."

"They're not intending to re-open the mine," Jerry said, trying to be convincing. "They're just digging a basement for the new restaurant."

"But if they should happen to hit rock, and pull up some of the silver ore..." The boy was sounding almost desperate. "If the right people see it, they will want to start mining again, and if they do, all of Silver Spring will be destroyed."

"First of all," Jerry said. "How do you know there is silver ore where the construction crew is digging?"

"Calvin Henshaw."

"Who?"

"Calvin Henshaw. He was a Welch miner. He saw it when the mine was still operating, and he warned the company about cave-ins. He's one of the men buried in the last one."

"Is all this in that book?"

"If you mean *the journal*, no. It was purposely left out so that no one would ever try to get at it."

"But there must have been records kept by the mining company…"

"Smith and Hayden Mining Company was too embarrassed by their poor safety record and their failure to keep the mine open. They'd already lost many men in that mine, and the people were getting upset about it… said the company was nothing but a bunch of greedy murderers by sending men in there, just to get killed. So they just kept quiet about there being more silver in that mine and nobody really cared that it was closed."

"And everybody just forgot about it?" Jerry said.

"That, and because it was the tomb for three men, people showed their respect and stayed away."

"And that's how… what was his name? Oliver? How Oliver was able to stash the gold and silver in there without anyone knowing."

"Again, you're partly right. *Almost* nobody… one other person knew about his nightly trips to the mine entrance."

"Who?"

"The author of the journal that's locked in the Tanglewood safe. That's why Robin and Grant and Keith came looking for the treasure in the first place."

Jerry was somewhat baffled by all this information, but he was intrigued, too. "I don't know what I can do to stop the digging," he said. "I just work here."

"Just go to your friends and tell them what I have told you."

"Why don't you tell them?"

"They're more apt to listen to you... I'm a stranger." The boy pulled out a pocket watch. "Look at the time! You were gonna take a bath. You need to be at the Crystal Palace by six."

Jerry looked at his wristwatch. "Yes, you're quite right," he said. "But what makes you think they'll listen to me?"

"Tell them what I told you... *everything*... they'll listen."

27

There was just enough time for Jerry to pick up a cheeseburger and a *Coke* at the North Star on his way to the theater. He had become accustomed to eating on the go, so it didn't seem out of the ordinary to him to be licking his fingers as he entered the dressing room area, but Jeanie, the make-up girl only looked at him with disgust and tossed him a towel. "Will you at least wipe off the mustard and catsup before I have to touch that face?"

Jerry inspected himself in the mirror on her table. "Sorry," he apologized. "I didn't have time for a sit-down dinner tonight," he said as he wiped away the condiments.

"If Puck is gonna steal the show again tonight," Jeanie laughed, "We have to start with a *clean* face."

Jerry headed to his dressing room to change into costume. When he emerged Jeanie was waiting.

"I just climbed out of my luxury bath at my condo before I came here," he said in a theatrical flourish, and then sat in the chair. "So, other than the mustard and catsup, the face should be clean."

Jeanie giggled as she draped a protective smock around his shoulders. "Luxury bath? Condo? You mean a dip in the creek?"

"Precisely, my dear," he replied, and then he was serious again. "By the way... have you seen Kevin around here this evening?"

"No, I haven't. Why?"

"I really need to talk to him, so if you should see him, please tell him... okay? It's really important."

The curtain went up before a smaller crowd; it was Monday, and it was expected. But this audience was no less enthusiastic about the Shakespearean comedy than any of the rest had been. Fewer seats filled, but the applause was equally energetic.

Although Jerry's head was swimming in what he thought was very alarming news to be delivered to his employer, he managed to get through another performance with his usual allure. When he entered the stage from dark shadows during the final bows, it was quite apparent that this audience was very much in agreement with the review opinions in Sunday's newspaper. But he was glad the show was over; it had been a mental struggle.

When he entered the dressing room that he shared with a couple of the other actors, Adam Hall and Derek Collins, who played Demetrius and Lysander, the two young Athenian men caught up in the humorous love triangle, they were hanging the formal suits they wore for the last palace scene.

"Another great audience again tonight," Adam said.

"Yeah, they were," Jerry replied.

"You were awesome tonight, too."

"Thanks, Adam. So were you."

"But you seemed a little off at the start of the fight scene."

Jerry sat down at the table, gazed at himself in the mirror, and then began removing the make-up. "Yeah... I'm really sorry that I messed that up."

"Aw, don't worry about it. I don't think anyone in the audience even noticed. And besides... Derek screwed up his lines worse than you did."

"Hey!" Derek whined. "Give me a break. The light got in my eyes and I couldn't see what I was saying."

They all laughed.

"Well, anyway," Jerry said. "You did a good job of recovering."

Adam sat down beside Jerry to start his make-up cleaning process. He made eye contact with Jerry in the big mirror. "Do you believe in ghosts?"

Jerry's brow wrinkled in a puzzled frown. "I don't know... why do you ask?"

"Well... haven't you heard the rumors about the ghosts in Silver Spring?"

"Rumors?"

"Y'know... lots o' people are saying that there really are ghosts here. You weren't rehearsing with us yet when some of our stage props got mysteriously moved. Mr. Thurston said it was Simon, the owner of the original theater that was here."

Derek came to join the conversation. "And my friend, Debbie, works in the bakery across the street. She says they hear voices and tinkling glasses every once in a while. That place was a bar and gambling parlor—"

"And a whore house," Adam added.

"Well," Jerry said. "I... I guess I've heard about all that, but..."

"But... but you don't believe it?" Derek said.

"I don't know. I guess it's possible."

"I don't know, either," Derek said. "But I do know that I get kinda creeped out sometimes when I see a person out on the street dressed up in old clothes... and I know it's not one of us."

"Yeah!" Adam said. "Like that blond kid with the big yellow dog."

"And the dude in the cowboy get-up. He's kinda scary."

"Cowboy?" Jerry said. "I think I've seen him, too."

A knock sounded on the door.

"COME IN," all three called out in unison.

The door opened just wide enough for a head to pop in. "Hi, guys! Great show tonight," Kevin said.

"THANKS, KEV."

He briefly stared at Adam and Derek, clad only in their underwear and T-shirts. "Am I interrupting anything?"

"No," Derek replied. "Come in and close the door... you're letting in a draft!"

The make-up was all off; Derek and Adam were getting dressed; Jerry just sat there. The room wasn't large, and it would be easier for him to change once the other two were finished. And he was hoping for an opportunity to talk to Kevin alone.

"You two up to a soccer game next weekend?" Kevin asked, and then he added, "You're welcome, too, Jerry... if you play."

"I have to work all weekend," said Adam.

"Can't," added Derek. "I'm taking my girlfriend to Red Hawk on Saturday, and we have a family reunion on Sunday."

"And I'm not much of a soccer player," Jerry said.

"Okay," Kevin responded. "Well, maybe some other time."

"We're going to get some pizza," Derek said. "You and Jerry want to join us?"

"I'm not really hungry right now," Jerry replied.

"Me either. But thanks for the invite." Kevin knew Jerry wanted to talk.

"Okay. See ya tomorrow night." Derek and Adam left.

"Jeanie told me you *had* to talk to me... said it was something really important."

"Yeah... well... I *think* it is," Jerry said.

Kevin sat on one the chairs as Jerry started changing his clothes. "Does it have anything to do with why you ditched me at suppertime?"

"Hey... I wasn't trying to ditch you. I'm sorry if it appeared that way. I was just honoring someone's trust in me, that's all."

Kevin wasn't convinced. "The guy with you when you went to your camp?"

"That's what I have to tell you about."

"Okay... so let's hear it."

"It was really weird... sort of... he showed up earlier today while I was working in the new garden... said he had something urgent to tell me, but he wanted privacy."

"So you took him to your secret hideaway..."

"Yeah... well, that's the only place I could think of."

"Is he the fellow we saw at Tanglewood Friday night?"

Kevin asked.

"Yes, and he's probably the guy they've seen at the North Star."

"And I saw him at Abbey's construction site this morning, too."

"Well, that's kinda what our conversation was about."

"Abbey's?"

"Well, not exactly Abbey's," Jerry replied. "But about the digging."

"The digging! What—"

"Let me explain," Jerry said. "He seems to know an awful lot about old Silver Spring, and about the mining that went on here. And he knows about the treasure that your brother and Robin and Keith found."

Kevin seemed a little startled. "So, what was so urgent?" he asked.

"He said that there are tunnels and caverns under Silver Spring Main Street that could collapse if they start digging out that old mine again."

"But they're only digging a basement."

"I told him that," Jerry said. "But he's afraid they'll dig up some silver ore, and someone will get the idea to start mining operations again. If that happens, all of Main street—including the Crystal Palace—could cave in and be destroyed."

"Sounds kinda funky to me," Kevin said.

"You wouldn't think so if you'd heard it from him."

"So, is that it? How do we know he isn't some nut case?"

"I don't know, Kevin. But he sounded pretty serious, and he knew too much detail about it, and about how your brother and his partners found the gold and silver. And he also said that if I told them *everything,* they would listen."

Kevin leaned back and stared into the wall a long moment. "I s'pose you *could* tell them. Do you *want* to tell them?"

"I don't know… do you think I should?"

"Do *you* think you should?"

"Yeah, I think so," Jerry said, almost in a whisper.

"Then why don't you stay at my place tonight, and we can be at their early morning meeting in the saloon."

"They have meetings in the saloon?"

"Every morning."

28

Rarely anyone other than Robin, Grant, and Keith attended their early morning meetings. It was a time for them to discuss privately their mutual business affairs; there was no secretary to take notes; there was no one to pass on information that they didn't necessarily want public. Silver Spring wasn't officially a municipality; it was a business—*their* business—and although they sometimes would seek outside advice and assistance, internal matters were kept in strict confidence between them.

Kevin knew the rule that no outsider should set foot in the saloon during the morning meetings without an invitation. He wasn't considered an outsider; he had been a part of this elite group since he was old enough to tag along with them to play in the park, and he had been a member on some of the earliest expeditions to Silver Spring, albeit a much less active role that he played then. But he had learned early on the value of privacy among this alliance; his respect for that value had earned their trust in him.

Jerry Stevens, however, was not an approved and accepted member, even though he had become a valued employee and close friend to Kevin. The trio of partners was aware of his delicate family issues, and they respected his privacy in that matter; in return, they expected the same consideration from him.

So Kevin knew he had to first request Jerry's presence at the meeting; he was confident that Robin, Grant, and

Keith would be interested in hearing the information he would offer.

"Jerry has talked with another of our mysterious visitors," Kevin began. "And he has learned some alarming news that I think is important for you to hear."

"What kind of *alarming* news?" Robin asked.

"That Silver Spring is in danger of being destroyed."

"What?" Keith exclaimed. "That's ridiculous!"

"Maybe," Kevin said. "But he told Jerry facts that he couldn't have known..."

"What kind of facts?" Robin asked.

"Like details about the mine tunnels and about how you found the gold and silver ingots."

"Who is this mysterious visitor?"

"Jerry thinks he's the boy from the North Star... y' know, the one who nobody has ever been able to talk to? He was here in this room the night of the cast party. I saw him, too, but I never got a chance to confront him."

"Where's Jerry now? Can you find him? Maybe we should hear what he has to say."

"He's right up in the apartment," Kevin replied. "I invited him to stay here last night after the play. It was late, and he seemed a little troubled, and I thought it would be better for him to stay here than to go back out in the woods."

"So that's why you were sleeping on the couch this morning," Keith said.

"Yeah, I let Jerry have my room."

"Well, get him down here," Robin said. "Let's hear what our *mysterious visitor* had to tell him."

Kevin had awakened his guest right after Keith had left the apartment; by now there had been enough time for him to shower and get dressed. Jerry was sitting on the couch waiting.

"Did you sleep okay?" Kevin asked.

"Like the proverbial rock," Jerry replied. "That's the first bed I've slept in for a long time. And I really appreciated the shower... thanks, Kevin."

"You're welcome. Are you ready to tell your story to the guys?"

"Do they want to hear it?"

"Absolutely... let's go."

This wasn't Jerry's first visit to the saloon; he had been there several times, but he was still impressed by its authentic retro appearance.

"Good morning, Jerry," Robin greeted. "Please, sit down. I've been admiring your garden artistry over in the Square—a striking welcome to all our visitors."

"Thank you," Jerry said. "It's the biggest horticulture project I've ever done."

"And, I might add, we are grateful to you for your contribution to the theater group. The show might've been cancelled if you hadn't joined them."

"Well, I knew the part already, and so it worked out."

"Kevin tells us that you've had an encounter with one of our unexplained visitors."

"Unexplained?   Is that what you call them?" Jerry chuckled.

"Until we find out who they are and why they're here."

"Okay... well, yes, I did talk to *someone* yesterday."

"Did you get his name?" Robin asked.

In all the excitement and confusion of Jerry's contact with the stranger, he now realized that he had failed to ask the boy's identity. "N-no. I guess I forgot to ask, and he didn't volunteer."

"That's okay... you'll remember the next time you see him. What did you talk about?"

"Well, actually, he did most of the talking and I listened. He told me that Silver Spring could be destroyed..."

"Destroyed? How?"

"He said there's a whole network of mine tunnels and large caverns under the town... where the silver was taken from... and that the three of you only saw a very small portion of it when you were searching for the treasure."

"How could he know that?" Grant piped up.

"He said the cave-in that stopped you from going any farther was the reason that you only saw part of it... and that there's a lot more. The caverns are right under Main Street, and they're huge."

"We saw some of the caverns," Keith said. "And I suppose there could've been others who saw them at one time or another, too."

"So why does that put Silver Spring in danger?" Robin asked.

"He's afraid that the digging for the restaurant will reveal the silver ore that's still there. If someone sees it, they might want to resume mining, and the caverns under the town could collapse. The Crystal Palace and all of Main Street would be destroyed by the cave-ins."

"Did he tell you how he happens to know there's silver ore?"

"He said a Welch miner named... um... Henshaw! Calvin Henshaw saw it when the mine was still operating. He warned the mining company of possible cave-ins... and he's one of the miners buried in the cave-in that you saw."

Robin looked at Grant and Kevin. They all remembered

the crosses placed upon the rubble in the mine tunnel. "Do either of you remember seeing that name in the journal?"

Grant and Keith thought a moment, and then they both shook their heads.

"He said a lot of that information was purposely left out of the journal... so no one would try to start mining again."

That startled Robin. "He knows about the journal?"

"Yes. He mentioned it a couple of times... in reference to other things."

"What other things?" Robin asked.

"About a guy named Oliver who stole the gold and silver from the smelter and hid it in the old mine where no one would find it. But, he said there was one other person who knew about Oliver's nightly trips to the old mine."

"Who? Who was the other person?"

"His exact words were: *the author of that journal that's locked in the Tanglewood safe.*"

Robin, Grant, and Keith all stared at Jerry with astonished curiosity. Then they looked at Kevin.

"Kevin. Have you told him any of this?" Robin asked, a little irritation poking through his words.

"No!" Kevin replied. "I never remembered any of it myself."

"He's telling you the truth," Jerry interrupted. "All Kevin ever told me was that you found the treasure in an abandoned mine... that's all. The nameless boy told me all the rest."

"Well," Grant said. "There's nothing he's said that proves any validity to any of this."

"Oh," Jerry added as an afterthought. "There was one other thing that... well, he said I should tell you *everything* he said... so you would believe... well, it might not be important, but he said you guys had some help in finding the gold and silver."

"Help?" Robin said. "We didn't have any help. It was just us."

"The boy told me that Keith used a walking stick to test a stream of water you had to cross. It scared you when it fell over while you were in the cavern. But it made Robby... he called you Robby... it made Robby think to use the stick to test the pool of water where you then found the ingots."

Now Jerry had their full attention. Robin eyed Grant and Keith again with a sizzling stare. "Did either of you *ever* mention that to *anyone*?"

Grant or Keith didn't have to think about that. "NO!" was their immediate answer.

"We were the only ones in that mine shaft," Robin said. "How could anyone *possibly* know about that?"

Kevin finally joined the conversation. "Apparently, you *weren't* alone in there."

"That's what the boy said, too," Jerry added. "He said the stick had a little push to make it fall."

29

Kevin and Jerry excused themselves and went about their work routine while Robin, Grant, and Keith continued their meeting. Now a new concept in the dynamics of Silver Spring suddenly presented more options to be considered for its growing future. Was there really silver ore in the earth beneath the village? Was there a feasible method of finding out? Would digging it out be worth risking the possibility of a disaster?

"First," 'Robin said, "We have to determine to what degree we can rely on the information that Jerry has given us." He hesitated, waiting for some response from Grant and Keith. When none was volunteered, he asked for it. He himself had been privately digesting the story, and he had inconclusively formed some opinions; he was hoping that Grant or Keith might say something to support his theory. "What is your first reaction to Jerry's claim?"

"I don't know what to make of it," said Grant. "I don't know the guy that well, but the details he knew about the walking stick in the mine shaft... well... that sort of blew me away."

"Me too," Keith said. "I've sorta gotten to know Jerry a little bit, only because of Kevin. Kevin seems to really like Jerry, and so far, there has been no reason to distrust him. And *really*... how could he make up something like that... something that is so dead-on true? He's not from around here, so it's not likely that he knew anything about us or Silver Spring before he came here."

"I agree. Who do you think told him all this?" Robin

asked.

"Whoever it is," Grant offered, "He knows us by name, and it sounds like he knows the history of Silver Spring."

"And why has he picked Jerry, of all people, to tell this stuff to?" Keith added. "Wouldn't it make more sense to come to one of us? Like Grant said, he seems to know us pretty well."

"Maybe he's afraid of us," Robin said. "Or maybe he wants to keep his identity concealed for some reason. And that reminds me... Keith... remember Sunday morning? I said I would check with Bill at the Wellington Daily News about that reporter, Tom Hargrove?"

"Yeah," Keith replied. "What'd you find out?"

"Bill has never met the guy in person, but he sees articles authored by *Tom Hargrove* now and then that just show up at their office. He thinks someone is dropping them off when no one happens to be at the front desk... like he's watching and waiting for the opportunity."

"What are the articles about?"

"Usually Silver Spring tidbits, but this play review is the first one they've actually printed. Bill said he couldn't resist, because it was such a good piece."

"It *was* good," Keith said. "It was excellent!"

"So, do they have a cell number... or an address?" Grant asked.

"Yes," Robin said. "Two-thirty-four North Johnson, 5Silver Spring."

Keith's eyes narrowed to slits, as if straining a thought.

"That's the address for our print shop... where the old newspaper office was," Grant said.

"Exactly. Bill said they checked to make sure it was a legitimate address, and of course, it was, so they printed the review."

"Why would this guy—*whoever* he is—use that address?" Keith pondered.

"Beats me to a pulp," Robin said. "I checked with the guys at the print shop and they don't have a clue, either. But they did say there had been some strange sounds... like distant voices and footsteps in there lately."

"Could our replica buildings of old Silver Spring *really* be attracting the *ghosts* of old Silver Spring," Grant said.

"Well, considering that we know there are spirits in Tanglewood..."

"So what should we do about the possible mining?"

"I suppose..." Robin paused a moment in thought. "I suppose we can call in an expert to do some tests."

"And what if there *is* something there?"

"Maybe Silver Spring will become a mining town again."

"But," Keith objected. "What if there really is a danger of the cave-ins? Like the boy told Jerry."

"A silver mine could be *quite* profitable, Grant said."

"So is the Crystal Palace. Are we going to risk that and the rest of the town on an ore deposit that might not pay off?" Keith argued.

"The risk is pure speculation. How can that boy know that there even *is* a risk of a cave-in?"

"He knew about the walking stick, didn't he?"

Keith's connection to the Crystal Palace Theater and the other buildings of their embryonic village was more passionate; although he didn't physically build them, those structures were his creations. He had spent countless hours at the drawing board nurturing the designs, interpreting the narrative descriptions from Clancy Crane's journal and searching through archives of historic architecture. He hated the thought of doing something—*anything*—that would jeopardize the health of Silver Spring.

"Keith has a good point," said Robin. "Let's not get too carried away with this until we know the facts. In the meantime, Russell Abbey's restaurant construction will continue; we can't stop his progress."

"And besides," Keith said. "I'm anxiously waiting for one of his Ranch Burgers... without driving to Wellington to get it."

After the meeting, Keith didn't waste any time getting to the construction site where the digging continued. Two dump trucks waited near the now growing rectangular hole that was to be a basement. The trucks were hauling away the removed soil, so there was very little piled up on the site.

Dave Parish greeted Keith. "G'morning."

"Mornin' Dave. How's the project going?"

"If we don't hit bedrock we should be done digging by this afternoon, and we'll start building forms tomorrow. I've ordered the concrete trucks to be here next Monday. Weather forecast looks good for the next week, so yeah, it's goin' good... right on schedule."

"You said *'If you don't hit bedrock.'* What are the chances?" Keith asked.

"I'd say right here... about fifty-fifty. We'll know in a little while 'cause we've only got a couple more feet to go."

Keith stepped closer to the edge and peered into the hole. This was the first of his Silver Spring projects that had required such extensive digging; none of the other replica buildings had basements under them. "I'd prefer that you didn't blast into any bedrock," Keith told Dave.

"Then we'd have to leave more of the basement walls exposed above ground."

"That would be okay. Just backfill around it so the bare concrete doesn't show," Keith suggested.

When Keith looked up from studying the bottom of the gaping hole, he noticed another spectator on the other side. It was that boy again, still monitoring the excavation with a concerned expression. At his side were another blond-haired boy and a large yellow dog. Keith thought of walking over to him and starting a conversation. But then he remembered Robin's comment that maybe the boy was afraid of him; if he tried to make personal contact, he might ruin the chances of all communications, even through Jerry.

The boy seemed to be aware of Keith's observation; he returned the stare a few moments, turned to walk away, and then he, his friend, and the dog disappeared around the back corner of the Crystal Palace. Keith was sure that was the last he would see of them that day, so after a brief chat with Dave Parish, he just returned to his office.

But that wasn't the last contact from the boy for someone else; soon after his noon lunch break with Kevin, when Jerry returned to his work in the Market Square garden, the two boys and the dog were waiting for him, lounging in a fairly obscure spot among some shrubbery. Their rather sudden presence startled Jerry. "Jeez! I didn't expect to find somebody in these bushes," he said when he happened onto them.

"Sorry," the boy said. "We didn't mean to scare you."

"Well, you did. What are you doing here?"

"Are you angry? Don't you want to talk to me any-more?"

"No... no, I'm not angry," Jerry replied. "I'm glad you're here. You just took me by surprise, that's all."

The two boys stood and the big yellow dog nuzzled Jerry's hand, soliciting some attention. Jerry stroked the fur on his neck.

"Did you tell your friends about the digging?" the boy asked.

"Yes, I did."

"Did you tell them everything?"

"Yes," Jerry said. "Even the part about the walking stick. That sorta freaked 'em out."

"But they're still digging over there," the boy said, sounding a little disappointed.

"But it's only a basement," Jerry said. "I don't think they'll get deep enough to find any ore. Robin, Grant, and Keith are good people; I don't think they would do anything to jeopardize the well-being of Silver Spring... especially something so foolish as to let the Crystal Palace and all of Main Street fall into a hole in the ground."

"I just have to be sure," the boy said. "This place means a lot to us."

"Don't worry," Jerry replied. "Silver Spring is in good hands."

"Well, let us be gone, then," the blond-haired boy said. "Your friend has spoken honorably, and therefore we should trust his words. Let us be off on another journey to seek adventure in the unknown land before us."

Jerry smiled at the boy's theatrical spiel. *He'd make a good actor,* he thought.

"Okay, then," the first boy said. "I'd like to visit you

again sometime soon, okay?"

"Sure. Anytime… except the next three nights… the play, y' know."

The two boys grinned and waved. "So long for now," they said, and strolled off. The big yellow dog, though, remained at Jerry's side, thoroughly enjoying the petting.

The blond-haired boy turned to call him. "Here Duke… c'mon boy!" The dog licked Jerry's hand and then ran after his master.

30

Kevin returned to the apartment at about five o'clock. He was tired; he hadn't gotten a full night's sleep, and it had seemed like an unusually long day. He kicked off his shoes at the door and flopped onto the sofa, relieved that he could possibly avoid the crowd of people already gathering for the Crystal Palace show.

"Hungry?" Keith asked as he emerged from his bedroom down the hall. "I'm meeting Robin and Tanya at the North Star... gonna try their prime rib special. Care to join us?"

"If it doesn't involve physical labor or coming in contact with more than three people."

"Rough day?" Keith asked.

"Just long... and not enough sleep last night."

"Well, unless you consider slicing a steak knife through prime rib as physical labor, I think you're safe. As for the three people... well, I can't guarantee that."

"Okay, but I need to take a shower first. And can I borrow a shirt that isn't wrinkled?"

Kevin was quite pleased to ride to the hotel in Keith's Grand Prix; the walk from Tanglewood to the other end of town would have completely drained what little energy he had left. He was glad, too, that Robin and Tanya were there waiting in the lobby and that they were all seated at a table in the North Star dining room immediately. It felt good to sit down.

When everyone was settled in and drinks and appetizers were ordered, Robin couldn't resist commenting on Kevin's attire. "Kevin! You're wearing a *pressed* shirt! Have you reformed?"

"I borrowed it from Keith," Kevin mumbled.

"Well, it looks very dashing on you." Then, to abruptly change the subject, Robin asked, "Did you talk to Jerry any more today?"

"Yeah, I saw him just before he left for his campsite at three," Kevin replied. "And guess what! He said he saw the boy again today, and there was another boy with him... a blond-haired boy, and a dog. Sounded like the boy you saw, Tanya."

"Tall and thin... and cute?" Tanya blushed.

"Must be the same one."

Just then the waiter came to their table.

"Good evening, everyone," he said with a smile. "My name is Mark and I'll be your waiter tonight. Are you ready to order?"

"Yes, I think we've all decided," Robin said. "We're all having the prime rib with baked potatoes."

"Excellent choice," Mark said. "I'll get that order in for you right away."

The waiter hustled away. Robin turned to Kevin. "Does Jerry ever talk to you about his family?"

"Not much."

"Did he ever tell you what happened?"

"You mean about the accident? Only that he was driving and his brother was killed. He doesn't remember any of it... only what he's been told, and he really doesn't want to talk about it."

"Did he think that quitting school and running away

from his family was going to solve anything?"

"Look... all I know is that he and his family didn't get along too good after that. His parents were taking it pretty hard, and Jerry's personality changed for the worse—so he says—and it was a mutual agreement between them that he should just stop spending time with them."

"He didn't just stop spending time with them, Kevin," Robin said. "He cut off all contact with them... entirely. He simply disappeared. They even filed a missing person report with the police."

"The police? Hey, how hard could it be to find him? He's been living right out in the open... well, sort of... and using his real name... it's not like he's some kind of criminal or fugitive or something."

"No, Kevin, he's not a fugitive from the law. His only crime is that he's causing a lot of worry for his family."

"He just needs some time to get himself straightened out," Kevin said.

"Straightened out?" Robin questioned. "What's so wrong with him? He seems quite normal to me."

Kevin scanned the area around them to make sure no one was eavesdropping. He leaned into the table and lowered his voice. "Jerry is kinda messed up about killing his brother and not remembering."

Robin leaned into the table, too. "Is it because he really doesn't remember? Or is it because he *doesn't want* to remember?"

"Well, whatever it is... it's *his* business. Hey... why all the questions about Jerry all of a sudden?"

"I received a phone call today," Robin said.

Kevin just stared, as if he knew he was going to hear some bad news.

"It was Jerry Stevens' father, Arthur."

"How did he know to call here?" Kevin asked.

"Up until now," Robin explained, "They hadn't widened their search beyond the Chicago vicinity. They didn't think he'd actually leave that area. But it seems that Virgil Thurston has a professor friend at Northwestern, where Jerry attended. Virgil mentioned Jerry to his friend on the phone, and the professor must have contacted Jerry's parents."

"So what's gonna happen now?" Kevin asked.

"They're coming here to see him. And it would surprise me if they don't try to convince him to return to Illinois with them."

"Can they *make* him go... if he doesn't *want* to?"

"No. He's an adult. If we find out there's something else... like evidence of abuse, for example, we have legal ways to protect him."

"I'd hate to see him persuaded to do something he doesn't want to do."

"Then maybe you should talk to him. You know him better than anyone else does."

"After the play closes," Kevin said. "If he hears this now, it could really screw up his performance."

"After the play closes won't be soon enough," Robin said.

"Why? When are they coming?"

"They've booked a charter plane... they'll arrive in Wellington on Thursday afternoon."

31

With only three performances of *Midsummer Night's Dream* remaining, Virgil Thurston made an important announcement backstage just before the Tuesday night show: "Jeffery Middleton has extended an invitation to the entire cast and crew for a closing night party, to be held at the North Star's banquet room after the final show."

A variety of responses indicated that almost everyone was in favor.

"It will be a reception as well," Virgil continued. "You will be meeting the public, shaking a lot of hands and hearing their personal sentiments."

"So, when it's over, it won't really be over," Adam Hall said.

"Do we have to stay in costume and make-up?" someone else asked.

"No, you don't have to," Virgil replied. "But that's up to you."

Jerry didn't feel any emotions either way about the party; he knew he would be meeting countless strangers, faces without names, people he did not know. Compared to the other actors and actresses in the cast who were well-known in the community and who would attract all the attention, he would probably have little involvement with fans who would actually show up at such an event. He would be there simply as an act of courtesy, and in respect to Virgil Thurston and the rest of the cast. For now, he would focus on delivering three good performances.

Kevin could barely keep his eyes open during the conversation after the prime rib. He was too tired, and too troubled about the forthcoming confrontation between Jerry and his parents; he didn't want to attend the theater show; he just wanted to go home and slip off to dreamland. It was going to be impossible to avoid telling Jerry about the upcoming visit; Robin had delegated that task to him. But there was still a little time to stall, and perhaps after a good night's sleep he would be able to think more clearly on the matter. When his head hit the pillow, he consciously had little time to think about anything, for he was asleep within seconds.

By that time, Jerry was giving his best performance before an appreciative crowd. He had cleared his head of thoughts about tunnels and caverns and cave-ins and collapsing buildings. Like a true professional actor, his mind was focused on the magic of the stage, far from his work in the Market Square garden or backhoes digging basements or even the strange, nameless boy who had been offering his friendship.

But when the house lights slowly brightened during the final bows, Jerry was once again reminded of the strange encounters; standing along the back wall of the theater were several people. It seemed unusual, as there were more than enough empty seats to accommodate everyone.

Jerry zeroed in on a couple of them. The nameless boy and his blond-haired companion waved, and Jerry sensed that the wave was intended for him. He raised his right arm to return the gesture.

All the while he, Adam, and Derek were changing and cleaning off make-up in their dressing room, Jerry half expected Kevin to knock on the door again. Kevin hadn't missed a single show during the entire run. But there had been plenty of time for him to get backstage; apparently he wasn't going to show up.

"You gonna go somewhere for food tonight?" he asked his roommates.

"Yeah... to the North Star for some burgers. Wanna come along?"

32

"Jerry... I have to talk to you about something," Kevin said with an uneasy tone. "It's important."

Jerry stood back in the morning sunlight, admiring the lavish garden he had created. There was very little left to do to it—maybe a few landscaping stones here and there—but the shaping and most of the planting was done. "What d'ya want to talk about?"

"Can we get together after your show tonight?" Kevin asked. "We could go to the North Star for drinks or something."

"But I have to get up early—"

"Don't worry about that," Kevin said. "You can sleep in tomorrow if you want. I mean, this garden is about finished, right?"

So that was it, Jerry thought. Now that the center attraction—his beautiful garden—was near completion, there was no need for him on the payroll anymore. Kevin was going to hand him a pink slip. "Well, I suppose we could..."

"Great! I'll meet you backstage after the show."

"Okay... I'll see you then." Jerry watched Kevin ride away on the utility tractor.

The Silver Pick Saloon inside the North Star Hotel was moderately busy; besides the hotel guests, patrons were gathering there after their evening at the Crystal Palace. All the way there in Kevin's Jeep, Kevin had been complimenting Jerry on his performance that night, and how he was finally beginning to understand the plot of the play. Jerry saw it as a way for Kevin to soften him for the punishing blows that would follow once they were in the bar.

Kevin maneuvered the Jeep into a parking space not far from the front entrance. On the silent walk into the lobby and then to the barroom, Jerry hoped that Kevin would get right to the point and not make this a long, agonizing process. They each got a mug of draft beer from the bar and then found an empty table across the room.

"So, Jerry..." Kevin began and then hesitated. "I know this is something you're probably not gonna want to hear."

Jerry tried to relax, anticipating the news that he no longer had a job. He'd spent the whole day trying not to think about his meeting, but of course that had not been too effective. Now it was painfully obvious that Kevin had some bad news, and what was there other than a cut in the payroll? But what difference would it make? Jerry had been on the move for the past two years, going from one job to another, town to town, state to state. And it had all been by his own choosing.

"I had dinner here last night with Keith and Robin," Kevin said.

"Oh? How was it?"

"The prime rib here is great... but I was so tired, I went right home and to bed afterward. That's why I didn't come to the theater last night."

Jerry tried to be patient and polite. But he knew Kevin hadn't brought him there to apologize for missing last night's show.

"Anyway," Kevin went on. "Robin and I had a discussion about you."

Okay, Jerry thought. *Here it comes.*

"So, the thing is," Kevin continued. "Apparently your parents filed a missing persons report a long time ago. They've been looking for you. I don't know if you knew that."

The abrupt change in the conversation suddenly confused Jerry; he was expecting bad news, but certainly not this. "N-no... I didn't know that."

"Sure... I s'pose if they didn't find you, there's no way you could've known."

This was not what Jerry was anticipating. "I... I... Jeez, Kevin, this is *not* what I thought you wanted to talk about. I thought it was gonna be about me leaving."

Now Kevin was confused. *"No!"* he said with a surprised expression. "You're not leaving, are you?"

Jerry felt the tension gripping him a little tighter. "Now that the garden is about finished... and the play will be closing tomorrow night... I suppose you don't have much need for me anymore."

"Don't be ridiculous! That's the farthest thing from my mind. Whatever gave you that idea?"

"I don't know... I just thought..."

"Well you thought wrong. We've got another project for you, and Virgil told me he hoped you would still be around for their next play in the fall."

"Really?" Jerry said.

"Yes, really."

"And what's the new project?"

"The resurrection of our pathetic little park over by the bluff. I've been working on it some, but you seem to have a knack for stuff like that."

"Okay," Jerry replied. "But what's the deal with my parents? How did that come up?"

Kevin took a deep breath and exhaled. He sipped his beer. "You told Virgil that you attended Northwestern. He has a professor friend there... someone he went to college with. He evidently talked to his friend on the phone and mentioned you. The friend remembered you as one of his students, and apparently he contacted your parents."

Jerry eyed Kevin with a puzzled stare. "So, how did you find out about all this?"

"Robin got a phone call yesterday," Kevin said.

"From who?"

"Your father. I guess it wasn't hard for him to locate you once he knew where to look."

Jerry sat silent, staring at his beer mug, his expression rather blank.

"They're coming here to see you," Kevin went on. "Robin thought I should give you a heads-up."

Jerry's expression remained quite neutral, as if he were feeling no emotion at all, but Kevin knew he *had* to be feeling *something*. "Are you okay? Say something."

"Of course I'm okay," Jerry said. "This just took me by surprise, that's all."

"Is there any reason why you don't want to see them?"

Jerry shrugged his shoulders. "It's... it's been a long time... over two years. I'm not sure if I even know them anymore."

"Well, maybe this will be a good time to get reacquainted, and I'm sure they will see the respectable person you are now."

Jerry looked Kevin in the eyes. "There are many things that I have learned about people and about myself in the past two years... people can forget the things you did; they can forget the words of anger that you might have spoken;

but they will *never* forget the way you made them feel."

"Jerry… I don't know what kind of person you were two years ago, but I *do know* what you are now, and if you show them the person you are now, how could they not like what they see?"

"My father can be very vindictive. He's wealthy. He uses his wealth to manipulate, and he's quite possessive; he treats other people like pawns in a chess game. Hell, he bought my way out of jail and…"

Jerry's words trailed off. He realized too late that he had gone past the limits. Now Kevin was standing on the edge of discovery, and he was bound to ask more questions. Jerry had not lied to him, so far, about his past; he just hadn't told the whole truth.

"But…" Kevin paused, thinking about what he had just heard. "But according to Robin, your father didn't sound like that on the phone. Robin said he sounded pleasant… and concerned about you."

"To Robin, maybe, but to me it will be different. You don't know my father."

"You said that you don't know him anymore, either… didn't you? Maybe your absence has made him change. People can change, you know. Look at yourself. According to what little you have told me about yourself, you have changed. And so could he."

"My guess is…" Jerry said and then hesitated as flashbacks of his life in a family environment invaded his thoughts. "My guess is that he will still think he owns me, like a piece of furniture, or a car, or a skill saw."

Kevin tried to be diplomatic. "If your father kept you from going to jail, perhaps you *do* owe him a bit of gratitude."

"Gratitude? Kevin... I would've gladly paid my debt to society. Perhaps I deserved to spend some time behind bars. I killed my brother by doing something stupid, senseless, irresponsible. But my father didn't hire that expensive lawyer to save *me*. He did it to save *himself*. To save himself from the embarrassment of having a son in prison. He couldn't handle that, and he told me so."

"May I ask why you were on the doorstep of a jail cell?"

"Drugs," Jerry said with remorse. "The night my brother died in that car crash, I was high on some junk I bought on the streets of Chicago. I was young and foolish. I didn't know any better... a nobody trying to keep up with the big wheels... and then..." He couldn't go on. His eyes pooled up tears.

Kevin reached across the table and gently clutched Jerry's forearm as a friendly gesture. "But it's all behind you now. It's time to move on and focus on what you've got *now*, and from where I'm sitting, it looks like you've got a lot going for you."

Jerry wrestled his arm away from Kevin's grasp and wiped his eyes with a bar napkin. "Yeah, sure," he said with a little sarcasm.

Kevin thought he could understand Jerry's position a little better now. Kevin came from a sound family with high moral standards; a father who he admired and respected, a mother who he cherished, and a brother who had, in his own way, always protected him and never let him down. But it wasn't difficult to imagine a life that was not privilege to all those qualities.

"I know this will be hard for you," Kevin said. "Just remember... I'll do anything in my power to help you through it... that is... if you *want* my help."

Jerry forced a little smile from behind his reddened eyes. "So... do you know when they're coming? I suppose I'm gonna have to face them sooner or later... as long as they've found me now."

"They're flying into Wellington on a chartered plane... they'll arrive tomorrow afternoon. And Robin said he gave your dad the number to this hotel to make a reservation."

"Tomorrow?" Jerry said. "But I have the play tomorrow night... and—"

"Yeah," Kevin interrupted with a grin. "Give 'em your very best performance."

33

Regardless of Kevin's suggestion to sleep in Thursday morning, Jerry showed up only a half-hour later than usual. He'd given some thought to not showing up at all—to pack up his few belongings and disappear into the wilderness, or catch a bus to somewhere. Anywhere. But that would be unfair to all those who had accepted him here, and who had treated him with certain dignity. He appreciated that, and he knew he couldn't just walk away from them. And it would be unfair to himself; Jerry had found a quality of life here that he had always believed was something only seen in the movies. The Chicago suburbs would never appeal to him again.

Yet, he knew that within a few short hours his self-proclaimed exile was about to be tarnished; he was no longer invisible; he had been found. His manipulative father would surely attempt to shame him into leaving with them; he would try to drag his son back to a life that would be neither healthy nor productive. Jerry hoped and prayed that he would find the strength to resist. He would no longer refuse to communicate with his family, but he *wasn't* going back to Illinois. Not now.

"Let's go over to the park and take a look around," Kevin said. "You might get some ideas what to do out there... and then we can make a list of materials you'll need."

"Is this to be another garden like in the Market Square?" Jerry asked.

"No, I don't think so... just a nice picnic area and a

scenic overlook… but it needs your magical touch."

As they walked the quarter-mile distance from the maintenance garage out to the park area, Kevin asked, "Are you nervous about your parents coming?"

After a moment's thought Jerry replied, "Not nervous, really, but it does feel strange… something I can't exactly explain."

"It won't affect your performance tonight, will it?"

"No. if I could block out the thought of Silver Spring falling into a big hole in the ground last night, I'm sure I can block out two people sitting in the audience tonight."

"Are you gonna see them before the show?"

"Depends on when they get here."

"Robin said they're supposed to land in Wellington about one o'clock."

"So by the time they get their rental car and get out here, it will be two, and I can't imagine my father wasting any time hunting me down."

They reached the park area; Kevin started explaining the improvements he thought should be made. "There should be a fence or a rock wall along the edge of that cliff," he said. "But we can have a contractor do that. Maybe a few trees and bushes… and some flowers wouldn't hurt. And of course, a few more picnic tables and benches… whatever you think."

Jerry pondered a few moments, gazing around the area. "If the fence or wall is for safety purposes, I have another idea."

"What?" Kevin asked.

"People will climb and crawl over a fence or a wall. But they wouldn't be so apt to climb over a hedge. A row of closely planted green shrubbery would be just as effective… maybe more."

"Good idea," Kevin said. "What else?"

"Will you open up this street for cars… so people can drive out here?"

"I s'pose we could. I'll suggest that to the guys."

"You really should let cars out here. It's too far from parking for people to walk, especially if they're carrying picnic baskets and coolers."

"Good point. Robin will agree with that."

With so much activity connected to the replication of a Nineteenth Century mining town, and with maintaining respectable levels of attention to their chosen professions as well, Robin, Grant, and Keith never had time to think about prospecting, much less, to give it any serious consideration. When they had made the decision to recreate Silver Spring several years before, mining hadn't even entered their thoughts. The town had suffered a slow and agonizing death more than a hundred years ago because residents of this place in 1899 were led to believe that the local mines had given up all they could give. There was no more. And for all practical purposes, that was true. When the town was destroyed, it was abandoned and forgotten as a once productive entity; it was scorned and avoided because of a credulous legend.

The "boys," however, treated it with more respect and attention to detail than anyone ever had. Of course, they discovered an advantage that no one else ever had—the journal. There was very little remaining recorded history about Silver Spring; much of it had been lost in the fires that completely destroyed the town, and in later years, anything still remaining was destroyed by the people who wanted to hide any truth. Little credence had ever been afforded to a diary kept by a young boy; had the journal been authored by an adult—especially a prominent citizen—it might have been taken more seriously. But Clancy Crane was just a kid, the young brother of a humble hotel keeper. Providentially for Robin Gladstone, Grant Kraemer, and Keith Bradley, when the diary was dismissed by the authorities as having little value, it was tossed aside, eventually buried in an attic under countless other materials collected by an old man. And of course, that old man was Robin Gladstone's grandfather.

As several perplexing events had occurred since the inception of new Silver Spring, Robin had once again returned to studying the old journal. It had been locked away for safekeeping; someday, Robin thought, it would be on display in the Silver Spring Museum. But for now, it remained in Tanglewood, its well-preserved parchment pages still providing clues to unlock the secrets of another time.

Now that the question of vast quantities of silver ore still lying under the streets was on the table, Robin was compelled to determine the validity of that claim. The unknown boy had told Jerry that a miner had seen the rich deposit, but there was no documentation anywhere to support his statement. How could this boy know about the miner's observation? He had also told Jerry that only one other person—the author of the journal—knew about Oliver Pratt's nightly jaunts to the abandoned mine. How could he know that? And most incredible of all, how could he know about the walking stick incident? But if he knew about that, a fact that all three of the partners knew to be exactly correct, how could they ignore the rest?

"We could call in a mining engineer team," Robin suggested. "They could drill test holes and collect samples."

Keith still wasn't in harmony with the whole idea. "I don't think we should do that."

"Why not?" Grant asked. "If there *is* something there, it could be a very lucrative venture."

"We're already in a very lucrative venture. Just look at all those people out there sightseeing and shopping... spending money in our stores, buying tickets to the shows in our theater... and we'll soon have plenty more attractions to draw people in."

"So what would be wrong with adding a mining operation to our portfolio?"

"For starters," Keith replied without hesitation. "Modern mining operations aren't the same as they were in 1890. It would ruin the atmosphere we've worked so hard to create. People come here for that... not to see and hear heavy machinery gouging away at our peaceful little hilltop. And let's not forget about the warning we've gotten about the possible cave-ins. I don't think I'm willing to take that risk."

"But we should at least find out if anything is there," Grant said.

"And then what? Sit back and watch our little piece of heaven crumble away? When it's all over... when the silver is all out, what have we got? Maybe a big hole in the ground. Certainly not our Silver Spring as we know it. What we have now will last our lifetimes. We should be thinking about protecting that."

"But from a financial standpoint..."

"From a financial standpoint? It's a big risk! What we have already... our little town that started out as just a hobby… something to have fun with… has become a sure thing. We have turned our little treasure hunt into a dynasty. Twenty years from now… when and if the people lose their romantic affinity for this place, when there are no more tourists, when there are no more shoppers in our stores, when there are no more shows in our theater… then… *maybe* I'll see fit to dig for more treasure, but for now, we should be happy with what we've got."

Keith presented a strong case against pursuing a mining operation at Silver Spring. His interest truly lay in the preservation of a historical place, not its destruction because of greed. For the first time he could remember since he and his partners had childhood disputes over such matters as who would play with the dump truck in the backyard sandbox, he was now running into opposition.

Robin didn't like to take sides. Keith and Grant were his best friends. Always had been. He sincerely hoped this issue could be resolved without creating hard feelings. So far, it was only discussion, and perhaps, with a little diplomacy, he could sway the outcome to an agreeable finish. "Let's not do anything right now," he said. "… Until we can gather some more information, and then we can sit down and draw some conclusions. Whatever is under our streets isn't going anywhere, so let's just give ourselves a little time to think this through."

34

Jerry checked his wristwatch frequently. Kevin had treated him to an early lunch at the North Star while they compiled plans for the park and a list of needed materials. Now he was back at the Market Square garden where he was finding room and transplanting the greenery previously residing in the corner of the Abbey's building site. As had become a daily routine, the unnamed boy and his companions, the blond-haired boy and his big yellow dog strolled by and naturally had to stop for a visit. The dog greeted Jerry with a cold nose nudging his hand, and then sat on its haunches and raised a paw offering a handshake. Jerry kneeled and took the paw in his right hand. "Hello, Duke," he said. "I heard your master call you Duke the last time you were here, so I guess that must be your name."

"R-r-r-r-r-ruff."

"What an oasis of splendid beauty you have created here..." said the blond-haired boy. "... Here in this otherwise barren land."

"Oh, I don't know about the barren part," Jerry replied. "The weeds seem to thrive quite nicely without my help." He gave Duke a good neck scratching, stood, and then offered his hand to the dog's master. "My name is Jerry," he said.

The boy vigorously shook Jerry's hand. "Edward, at your service, sire. I am most honored to make your acquaintance."

Jerry grinned. "And I am pleased to meet you, as well."

Then he turned to the other fellow. "As many times as we have met and talked, I still don't know your name." He extended his right hand toward the boy.

"M-my name is Clancy. I... I thought you knew," he said as he shook Jerry's hand.

Edward nudged his friend with an elbow and nodded toward Main Street. "We must take our leave... commence on our journey to conquer yet another horizon of the great unknown."

Clancy gazed briefly toward Main. "Yes, well... it's been nice talking to you," he said to Jerry. "We'll see you again soon." They waved and then they left.

A couple of minutes later, Kevin stepped into the garden beside Jerry. "It's time," he said. "Your folks are waiting for you in the Tanglewood saloon. They've been talking to Robin for a while."

Jerry hesitated outside the front floor at Tanglewood before going in. For just a moment he wished he would have invited Kevin to come with him, but that wouldn't be fair. Kevin didn't deserve such punishment.

Stalling wouldn't make the situation any easier, so he forced himself to open the door and entered the saloon. There they were. His mother sat at a table and his father stood behind her. After only two years, they looked so much older than he remembered. They just stared at him, and right away Jerry knew this might be more difficult than he had anticipated.

"Mom. Dad. Hi." Not exactly the first words he expected to hear in that room, but it was more than either of them were attempting.

Tears rolled down his mother's cheeks. He expected

that, just as he expected the stone-cold stare from his father. They still said nothing. Jerry decided he'd give it one more try, and if it didn't get them talking, he'd go hide in the maintenance garage. "So... Kevin said you've been... well... I didn't know you've been looking for me."

"Jerry," his mother finally spoke. But it sounded more like she was scolding. "How could you possibly think that we wouldn't?"

"Because you..." Jerry paused in a deep frown, reviewing in his mind the last time they had been together. Satisfied that he was remembering it correctly, and that he was not misinterpreting the memory, he went on. "Because our last conversation went something like *'Get out of our house,'* and my response was *'Okay... but don't come looking for me.'*" He suddenly realized that he didn't have the old emotions buried quite as deeply as he thought. He took a deep breath and continued. "You said I was destroying the family, and that I should leave."

His mother's voice matched her saddened expression. "We were upset, Jerry. We'd just lost a son, and you were frightening us."

"Jerry," his father said, trying to show some compassion, but his words were still icicles on a January rain gutter. "I think the more accurate phrase was *'We think you should move into your own place.'* We didn't mean you should run half-way across the country... and we're sorry you didn't understand."

There he goes, Jerry thought. *Trying to manipulate the scenario to his own advantage.* "But you sounded angry when you told me to leave."

"Perhaps we were... then."

"Oh," Jerry replied. "You were angry then, but now

you're not. Okay. So you've changed your mind. Fair enough. But you assumed that I should somehow just know that?"

The room was silent for a few moments; they had reached a stalemate. Neither side could win that argument. Jerry realized that a change in direction was necessary. "Okay… so we can't change the past. This is now. You came all the way out here. Why?"

"We came here looking for our son," his mother cried. "We were hoping to see some positive emotion from you. After all you put us through, wondering if you were dead or alive for so long… and now when we finally find you, you act as if we're an inconvenience."

"Mom. Dad. I didn't exactly see you come running with open arms when I came through that door, either."

"We didn't know what to expect," his father said.

"Mom. Dad. The son you cared about so much is dead. I killed him… remember? That's what you told me. Hell, I don't remember! I've been trying, but I don't. I don't think that I could've meant to hurt him, but I did. I killed the *only* one you cared about. So I guess you must've thought I did it on purpose."

His mother stood up and stepped toward him. She brushed away the tears. "That's not true! We cared about you, too, but Charles was a special child—you knew that— he needed more attention; he couldn't take care of himself, and you were so good at looking after yourself… and him."

Jerry's father remained somber and still. His wife looked at him as if she expected him to say something. But he didn't.

"Maybe it wasn't fair for us to put so much responsibility on you," she continued. "But you cared about him, too…

a lot. And sometimes we needed a break and we knew we could count on you. And don't ever think that we didn't love you."

Jerry was filing all this away to think about it later. He was proud that he had not raised his voice or allowed the conversation to get out of hand. Neither he nor his parents were in control, but it wasn't over. He feared that his father hadn't opened his arsenal yet. But he had to deal with it, and in the end, he hoped to save his dignity.

"I work here, now," he said after a long silence. "But I guess you already knew that,"

"Yes," his father finally said. "This is a very impressive place, although the owners are a lot younger than I expected."

"They're good people," Jerry said.

"And you're working as a gardener. You were working on your master's at Northwestern. Jesus! What the hell are you thinking... working as a gardener?"

There was the first stinger missile launched in his direction.

"Dad. If you recall, my master's is in biology—botany, to be more precise—so I am doing exactly what I want to do."

"But think of what you could be—"

"Dad. One of many things I have learned on my own is that it is better to think about what you are, rather than what you are not. Right now, I am a gardener. A gardener's life is pleasantly varied with the seasons and offers a chance for self-expression and creativity. It's a skilled craft."

"Skilled craft! Hmf." Arthur Stevens didn't seem impressed.

"I take it you haven't seen the Market Square garden," Jerry said. "While you were busy developing another one of your harmful herbicidal concoctions at that chemical plant where you spend all your time, I was creating a green space masterpiece. You should take a look at it before you leave."

"Yes… well… maybe we will. But Mr. Gladstone told us you're living in a tent out in the woods. What kind of a life is that?"

"As a matter of fact, it's a wonderful life. No phones; no utility bills; no mortgage payments; no nosey neighbors. I eat three square meals every day, and I sleep like a baby in the quiet, peaceful bliss of nature. Of course, if all that bothers you, it might comfort you to know that it's probably temporary."

"I'll say it's temporary!" his father growled. "You'll go pack up your belongings right now and go with us back to Chicago."

"Can't do that, Dad. I have a stage performance tonight at the Crystal Palace… or had you forgotten that's how you discovered my whereabouts?"

"Stage performance! So you're an actor in some two-bit silly play put on by a bunch of amateurs. Jerry, you need to forget about all this foolishness and focus your thoughts on going back to finish your degree."

Foolishness. That hurt. It was happening just as he suspected it would: his father was going to bully his way into total ownership of his son. But Jerry wasn't going to let that happen.

"Look, Dad." Jerry glanced at his watch. "First of all, I'm *not* going back to Chicago." He stared momentarily into his mother's eyes, and then his dad's. "You're staying at the North Star Hotel, right?"

Arthur nodded.

"I have to get ready for that *two-bit play*. Tonight is the final performance of seven. The last six have been a full house, but the hotel *might* have a couple of tickets for you. There's a closing night reception afterwards at the North Star. We can talk more then."

As Jerry left for his condo in the woods and his luxury bath, he wasn't absolutely certain that he had *complete* control of the entire situation, but he was confident in his own control. Even though he thought he should be feeling some sort of deep remorse, he didn't. His mom and dad had turned their backs on him over two years ago, at a time when he needed their help and understanding the most. But they were so wrapped up in their grieving and indulging in the pity from everyone in their social circles that they failed to recognize Jerry's cries for help. That was when he had turned to drugs—not in a recreational manner as had been his previous experience—but as an escape from the psychological torture his parents slammed on him. Luckily he caught himself before it was too late, realizing that drug abuse only worsened his status. At the final showdown, the day his father had told him to leave their house, Jerry saw his perfect opportunity to make a more effective escape—one that would save him from the spiraling fall he was in. So he left, never looked back, never missed what he had left behind.

35

On their way back to the hotel, Mr. and Mrs. Stevens thought they should tour the village, as they had nothing, now, but time on their hands. Arthur turned the rented Lincoln sedan toward the Market Square, following the sign that pointed to "Parking." He nosed the car into a space where two dozen people admired the garden in all its summertime radiance; many of the flower varieties were in full bloom, their clusters, rows, and geometric patterns gracing the sculpted and contoured stone-lined terraces that spiraled around mounds of earth. A hedge of low shrubs outlined the perimeter, guarding against intruders, and platoons of small trees and bushes stood as sentries, watching over the colorful residents within.

"Do you suppose this is the garden that Jerry mentioned?" Mr. Stevens said.

"I don't see any other," replied his wife. "It *is* quite remarkable, isn't it?"

Arthur didn't respond verbally, but she knew he was impressed.

Browsing along the boardwalks gave them a close-up look at the replica architecture that Robin had encouraged them to inspect. They had seen other similar tourist attractions, but none could compare to these functional stores offering practical merchandise other than picture post cards, over-priced hand painted shot glasses and monogram key chains. And in nearly every window they passed were various posters promoting the Crystal Palace presentation of *A Midsummer Night's Dream* starring *Jerry Stevens* as "Puck."

"Perhaps we should get back to the hotel," Arthur suggested.

"Yes," said Mrs. Stevens. "And make sure we can get tickets."

"There are only four tickets left," the desk clerk informed. "Are you guests here at North Star?"

"Yes... Mr. and Mrs. Arthur Stevens, room two-thirty-five."

"Ah, yes," the clerk said after checking the register. He slid two tickets across the counter. "Complimentary. Enjoy the show."

Arthur Stevens had envisioned a cracker box theater with a portable riser for a stage, maybe a piano, and three dozen metal folding chairs for audience seating. His chin probably had bruises from hitting the floor when they entered the finely appointed four-hundred seat arena. It was again a full house, but an usher escorted them to a couple of empty seats along the far right aisle.

They had just settled in when, promptly at eight o'clock, the house lights dimmed and a pleasantly strong, deep voice filled the air. *Ladies and gentlemen; the Crystal Palace Theater proudly presents to you the Wellington Players performing the Shakespearean comedy, A Midsummer Night's Dream.*

Hearty applause sounded as the curtain parted, revealing the lavish castle parlor scene and several actors entering the stage. Already, it was clear to Arthur Stevens and his wife that this was no back alley kids' show. But unfamiliar with the Shakespearean story, they were beginning to get discouraged, not recognizing their son as any character all through the first act. After the short intermission, however, more vigorous applause welcomed Jerry onto the stage as he opened Act Two, meeting an attractive woman dressed as a fairy with white silky wings and an abundance of sparkle. Jerry's boyish face was exaggerated with make-up, and his tight-fitting elf costume emphasized his muscular physique, raising quite a stir among the ladies in the audience. The Stevens couple didn't know whether to be proud or to be embarrassed.

By the end of the third act, they had forgotten all that; they'd had a few good laughs and were enjoying this tale of a star crossed love affair, accidently mixed up by the magical powers of a mysterious purple flower and a playful, mischievous spirit called "Puck." Jerry was at his best, as were all the performers. No one would leave the theater that night feeling cheated.

At the very end, all the stage lights dimmed except one spot at front center. Jerry casually walked from the shadows, stepped into the spotlight and sat on a bench, one foot on the floor and one on the bench, one elbow rested on his raised knee, dark silhouettes of castle spires looming behind him. He thought briefly about this being the very final performance—his last chance to recite Puck's farewell to the audience the way Shakespeare had originally intended. He knew the lines well, and he was certain that Mr. Thurston would eventually forgive him for deviating from the modified script this one time. He paused dramatically while the house became as still as a nursery at midnight. Then he turned his head toward the audience and began:

If we shadows have offended,
Think but this, and all is mended,
That you have but slumbered here
While these visions did appear.
And this weak and idle theme,
No more yielding but a dream,
Gentles, do not reprehend;
If you pardon, we will mend;
And as I am an honest Puck,
If we have unearned luck
Now to 'scape the serpent's tongue,
We will make amends ere long;
Else the Puck a liar call.
So, good night unto you all.
Give me your hands, if we be friends,
And Robin shall restore amends.

The one spot light slowly faded as Jerry stood and walked into the shadows again, disappearing into the darkened stage.

The silence suddenly erupted into thunderous applause that continued for several minutes until the stage partially brightened; the roar diminished as the crowd anticipated something more. But of course, what they saw next was the entire cast filing onto the stage forming a single line at the footlights, hand in hand, bowing in unison. Now everyone in the audience was on their feet, clapping, cheering and whistling. It was the longest ovation of the entire seven night run. And it was the last.

All the actors knew, however, that it wasn't quite over yet; they still had to meet their fans at the reception. Popular vote among the cast had decided to leave costumes and make-up in the dressing rooms at the theater. Street clothes would be more appropriate for the occasion. Virgil Thurston had suggested something with a little more class than faded blue jeans and T-shirts.

No one was allowed into the North Star banquet room until the stars of the show had arrived and were afforded a few minutes to get settled in. Not much settling in was necessary; they were all in high spirits, congratulating one another with clinking glasses, handshakes, and plenty of hugs. Mixed emotions raced among them; they were glad that it was over; happy that it had been a triumphant success; but sad that they would not all be together again.

As the doors opened and fans poured in, Jerry figured he could just as well find an obscure corner somewhere, as this was when all the people would gravitate to the local celebrities. Perhaps Kevin would show up, so at least he would have someone to talk to.

Kevin did show up, but it was quite some time until he was able to get close to Jerry; it seemed Jerry drew just as much, maybe more attention than the others. When Mr. and Mrs. Stevens saw the popularity their son had achieved, they kept their distance, giving him plenty of room, waiting until the crowd thinned out a little.

"That was a great show!" Kevin said. "You were awesome."

"Thanks, Kev. Did you understand it this time?"

"Yeah, I think I'm finally catching on."

Kevin stayed by Jerry's side while a constant parade of mostly unfamiliar faces offering Jerry and the others congratulations and handshakes. But one familiar face eventually worked his way toward Jerry. "That was a most interesting finish," Virgil Thurston said.

Jerry's face reddened just a little. "I... I... don't know what came over me. It just happened," he lied. He'd actually been secretly planning his surprise ending for two days.

"Well," Virgil replied. "It was a bit of a shock to me, but you pulled it off perfectly. I'm sure the audience thought it was just the way it should be."

"So, you're not mad?"

"Of course not. I wouldn't have thought to suggest such a variation, but in all honesty, Jerry, I think it was brilliant."

Kevin appeared quite confused. "May I ask what he did that was so brilliant and that you are not mad about?"

Virgil winked at Jerry. "You see? No one noticed." Then he turned to Kevin. "Jerry recited the lines of the final farewell just the way Shakespeare wrote it... not the way I altered it to modern language... like the entire rest of the play."

"Oh," Kevin said. "I thought it sounded... just fine."

The hour was getting late and the crowd dwindled rapidly. Jerry noticed his parents, smiled and waved. A few seconds later they were there. Jerry introduced his mom and dad, Arthur and Yvonne Stevens to Director Virgil Thurston.

"Pleased to finally meet you," Arthur said as he shook Virgil's hand.

"And this," Jerry continued with the introductions, "Is my best friend, Kevin. He's sort of my boss, too."

"Yes," Arthur said. "We met just briefly earlier today."

"Did you see the play?" Virgil asked the Stevens.

"We did," Arthur replied.

"And it was wonderful," Yvonne added.

Just then someone grasped Virgil's arm and whisked

him away to another group across the room. Jerry sudden-ly found himself feeling a little awkward.

"Well," Mr. Stevens uttered after a few moments of si-lence. "Would the two of you care to join us in the bar for a cocktail?"

Jerry knew he couldn't escape from the invitation. But Kevin could. But if Kevin was there, perhaps his father would be less pretentious, less condescending. He looked to Kevin with pleading eyes.

Kevin read the message clearly. "Sure," he responded. "But just for a little while... work in the morning, you know."

They found a vacant table in the busy lounge and or-dered drinks. Kevin was a bit uncomfortable with the situ-ation, but he thought Jerry seemed to need his alliance. He could give him that.

"Mom, Dad," Jerry began the converstation. "Did you have a chance to see the Market Square garden this after-noon?"

Mrs. Stevens nodded. "It's lovely..."

"Yes, we did," said Mr. Stevens. "It's very nice... but..."

Uh-oh, Jerry thought. He braced himself for his dad's criticism that was certain to be embarrassing. *But*... could only mean that one of his condescending remarks was im-minent.

"But I was wondering," Arthur went on, "Why didn't you ever do anything like that at home?"

That wasn't what Jerry was expecting. The zinger was surely to follow. "Um... because you don't have a two-acre parking lot with a huge garden in the middle?"

"No... but your mother has some very adequate flower beds."

"Those are *her* flower beds," Jerry argued.

Arthur realized that he was getting nowhere on the garden issue; it was time to change the subject. "So, have you reconsidered my offer?"

"What offer?"

"Coming back to Illinois."

"Dad. That wasn't an offer. It was an order."

"Call it what you want." Mr. Stevens turned to Kevin. "Jerry is working on his master's at Northwestern," he explained. "A most unfortunate accident interrupted his studies, but now he needs to return to it."

"Dad," Jerry said. "I'll go back to school. But I'm *not* going back to Chicago or to Northwestern. I'll finish my degree, but not there."

"But *I* graduated from Northwestern," Arthur said.

"That doesn't make it mandatory for me to do the same. If I go back there now, I'll only be tempted to fall back into the same mess I was in when I left. Please understand that. And please understand that I have found a better life here. This is where I want to be."

"A better life? Living in a tent and working as a gardener? You call that a better life?"

Lift-off! We have a zinger! "I am doing this because it's *my* choice... not someone else's." Jerry put his hand on Kevin's shoulder. "I have friends here who let me feel like I make a difference and who allow me to feel like a genuine person and who accept me for who and what I am. They don't expect me to be someone I'm not."

Kevin was beginning to grasp the concept that Jerry had tried to relay to him before; he sensed that Jerry was about to lose any family support that he might have had, only because Jerry didn't want to return to a chaotic lifestyle in the city. Jerry couldn't be faulted for that. He so wanted to defend Jerry, but he thought better of interfering in the family issues.

"Arthur," his wife said, laying her hand on his forearm. "Maybe we should let this rest a while. Dragging Jerry back to Illinois won't bring back Charles. Jerry suffered enough over that… and we didn't help matters any. He seems to be happy here, and maybe we should respect that."

"But I have a lot of money invested in his education. He shouldn't just ignore that."

So there it was… the money issue. "Dad!" Jerry said emphatically. "I'll go back to school. But *not* Northwestern."

"Where, then?"

"I don't know. There are a lot of schools. Maybe something out here. But right now, I'm very tired. I don't want to talk about it anymore tonight. I just want to go and get some sleep."

"You're going back out to a tent in the woods?" his mother gasped.

"No," Kevin intervened. "He's staying at my place tonight. He's staying at Tanglewood."

36

When they woke up Friday morning, Kevin insisted that Jerry should take the next couple of days off. "The garden will still be there, and you should spend some time with your mom and dad."

"I'm not sure that I want to do that."

"Why?"

"They'll keep nagging me to go back to Chicago."

Kevin thought a few moments. "You made it quite clear to them last night that you aren't going back. I heard it."

"Yeah, and I told them that yesterday, too, but they still kept on about it last night."

"Jerry, tell me... honestly... are you absolutely sure about your decision to stay here instead of going back home?"

"Yes," Jerry said without thinking about it. "I'm absolutely sure."

Downstairs in the saloon, the discussion about mining and the future for Silver Spring continued. Not much had changed in the past twenty-four hours; Grant still thought it should be investigated; Keith was still opposed to the idea; and Robin was still on the fence, considering both sides. He was the devil's advocate—his vote, either way, could cause dissention among them. None of them wanted that, but none were in favor of changing their own position.

There were other matters to discuss, so the mining question was set aside. "How'd we do at the Crystal Palace?" Keith asked.

"All the figures for the expenses aren't together yet," Robin said. "But ticket sales were just under twenty-eight thousand dollars. All nights were sold out except Monday. I think we'll clear about twenty grand. And if we give fifteen percent to the theater club, we'll still be seventeen thousand in the black."

"And how's the situation with Jerry and his parents?" Grant asked. "Is there going to be any trouble?"

"I talked with Mr. and Mrs. Stevens yesterday when they arrived," Robin said. "They're difficult to read; they seemed nice enough, but his father is quite domineering. His intentions are to drag Jerry back to Chicago."

"And if Jerry doesn't want to go back to Chicago?" Keith said.

"It's a family matter," Robin replied. "We don't have any right to interfere with that."

"But what if it gets dirty?"

"All we can do is to prevent bloodshed. I will step in *only* if it becomes a legal issue."

After fresh bagels, warm cinnamon rolls and lots of orange juice at the bakery, Kevin and Jerry talked about the new project at the park. "I'll order another truckload of nursery stock on Monday," Kevin said. "We should get it in about a week."

"How 'bout the road?" Jerry asked.

"Yup... they'll do that, after we're done with the rest of the work. Flatrock Street will go all the way out there from Main."

Kevin had to get on with his day; there was plenty to do in the theater getting ready for the weekend shows— Friday night, a concert pianist; Saturday and Sunday, Celtic singers and dancers.

Jerry sat alone at the table outside the bakery for a while. As soon as Kevin had left, his thoughts had turned to the family problem facing him; to what lengths his father would go to return him to Chicago, he did not know. And that's what bothered him now; he didn't know how to be prepared when his father started pulling aces from the bottom of the deck.

He decided to take a walk out to the park; perhaps trying to capture an image of the future layout and do a little mental planning would help him to temporarily clear his head. Sitting on the bench he imagined a row of arbor vitae along the edge of the cliff, trimmed square to resemble a low wall. At the very center of the park would be another colorful garden, like the one at Market Square, only much smaller, surrounded by more shrubbery. A small shelter gazebo would be good, and several redwood picnic tables...

"Aren't you working here anymore?" a voice interrupted his visions.

Jerry turned abruptly toward the voice. Just to the

right of the bench stood his new friend, Clancy. "Sure, I still work here," he said. "I was told to take the day off."

"Oh. What are you doing out here?"

"Relaxing... thinking about how I'll fix up this park."

"Are you gonna make another garden?"

"Sort of," Jerry replied. "But not like the Market Square."

"The school used to be right over there," Clancy said as he pointed to the north. "And there was a blacksmith shop right about here. And down that way..." he pointed back toward the village. "There was the book store and a bakery and a boarding house... right along Flatrock Street." Then he pointed to the cliff. "In the middle of that cliff is the entrance to the mine where Robby and Grant and Keith found the treasure."

Jerry jumped to his feet and started toward the edge.

"You can't see it from here. Don't try. It's a pretty long fall. But I can show you from down in the valley."

Jerry stopped and came back to the bench. "Okay... I'd like that. Let's go."

They spent the rest of the morning hiking down into the valley, along the creek, and through woods. Jerry got a good look at the mine opening a hundred feet up on the side of the sheer rock cliff and decided he didn't need to get any closer.

"You sure know a lot about Silver Spring," he said.

"It's a very special place to me, and to others, too." Clancy's face became quite somber. "I've spent many years thinking about how it used to be, and making sure nothing happened to it. And it would break my heart to see the mining start again. It would destroy Silver Spring forever."

"I think I know what you mean," Jerry replied. "I'd hate

to see that happen, too."

"Is that why you're looking so sad today?"

Jerry looked at his friend curiously. "Why do you say that?"

"You look sad. Something's bothering you."

"It's my father. He and my mom are here visiting, and they're trying to drag me back to Chicago, and I don't want to go."

"You love this place, don't you?"

"Yeah, I guess I do."

"So then you just have to tell them you're staying."

"Yeah, I guess I will."

37

Jerry knew he would have to face his father sooner or later. He might as well get it over with. If he made the first move, if he went to the hotel and confronted them, maybe he could gain a little more control. He ordered a chicken salad sandwich at the bakery, sat at a table on the veranda, and contemplated what he would tell them. As he ate his lunch, he noticed the familiar rented Lincoln pass by; it turned toward the Market Square. He gulped the rest of his sandwich as he walked briskly after it. Arthur and Yvonne were out of the car, admiring the garden by the time he caught up.

"Mom. Dad. I was on my way to the hotel to see you."

"Well, I'm glad we didn't miss you," Arthur said. "We're going into Wellington and maybe a little sightseeing of the countryside. We knew you were probably working, but we wanted to find you. Will you join us for dinner tonight at the hotel?"

Jerry looked at his father with great suspicion. This was surely another tactical maneuver to lure him back to Chicago and Northwestern. Reluctantly, he answered, "Sure. What time?"

"How's seven o'clock?"

"I'll be there."

"We're leaving tomorrow, you know."

Jerry waited for his father to ask if he was packed and ready, but the question didn't come. Evidently, that would be left for after dinner conversation.

The North Star dining room was nearly filled to capacity. Arthur Stevens announced his reservation to the hostess; she checked the list and then, with a smile, escorted them to a table. "Kim will be your waitress tonight," she said, and then offered to bring them drinks from the bar.

Jerry felt a little tense sitting across the table, looking at the two smiling faces looking at him. These were the two people he should love the most, and he did, but he had other feelings about them as well. He hoped his tenseness didn't show. He just had to stay calm, and remember his escape plan: if the battle zone became too hot, he would simply excuse himself for a bathroom break, and not return.

His tension eased a little, though, when Arthur launched the conversation into the topic of Jerry's involvement with the theater group.

"It just happened," Jerry explained. "One of the actors quit only two weeks before opening night. It was a part I knew."

They talked a while about the play and the theater while they waited for the steaks and lobster. When the food arrived, Yvonne Stevens turned the discussion to the stunning Market Square garden. Jerry told the story about how he had first met Kevin. "I was voluntarily caring for the flower planters on Main Street. It caught Kevin's attention and aroused his curiosity... and that afternoon he offered me a job."

All through dinner, dessert, and drinks afterward, Jerry kept expecting the surprise attack from his father; it had been almost twenty-four hours since the last one. So far, not one word had been spoken about his return to Illinois, continued education, living in a tent, or his dead brother. But something was in the air. Jerry could feel it.

"Jerry," his father finally said after a long silence. "Your mother and I have discussed at quite length your status here."

Uh-oh. Here it comes.

"We were quite amazed with that garden, and we were nearly knocked breathless last night sitting in the audience at the Crystal Palace watching your performance. And at the reception we saw the people gravitated to you and your interactions with the other actors, and it wasn't difficult to tell that you felt a sense of belonging."

Jerry heard something in his father's voice that he had never heard before. It was sincerity unlike the usual sternness in his lectures about respect and responsibility.

"So," Arthur went on. "We have come to the conclusion that you must really be happy here. You never were so happy in Illinois. We shouldn't deprive you of that. As much as we'd like you to come home, if this is where you want to be, we're not going to stand in the way."

Jerry sighed a breath of relief. He was shocked—but relieved.

"I do, however, hope that you will consider going back to college... somewhere."

"When I've saved up some money," Jerry said. "I can't afford it right now. But I will."

"Nonsense," Arthur replied. "When you've decided which school you want to attend, let me know and I'll make the financial arrangements. You may not know this, but I set aside funds for your education a long time ago. I guess it doesn't matter where the money is spent, just as long as you use it the way it was intended."

"So you're saying that I don't have to go back to Northwestern?"

"No, you don't have to go back to Northwestern."

The next morning, Jerry met his mom and dad for breakfast at the hotel dining room. This time he could feel more at ease, knowing they wouldn't badger him for wanting to stay in Silver Spring. It would be just a short visit, anyway; Arthur had arranged to meet the charter plane pilot at the Wellington Airport at nine o'clock. But it was long enough for Jerry to speak his true feelings to them.

"As much as you think otherwise," he began, "I've been living a good life here. I really wasn't trying to hide from you because I didn't think I had to. I thought you were happy I was gone. I know I've made mistakes and maybe I wasn't everything I should've been, but that doesn't mean I want to go back and start over." He wasn't sure if they understood, but they *were* listening. "I need some time, but I promise that I'll keep in touch. Is that good enough for now?"

"For now, that will have to do." His father smiled sadly. "Jerry, I'm sorry that I wasn't always there for you."

This wasn't what Jerry expected from his father. "No, Dad. It was mostly my fault. I was a mess and—"

"No, Jerry. We were at fault more... after Charles. If we made you feel uncomfortable, I'm sorry."

"Jerry," his mother joined in. "We know we neglected you then, and we want to make it up to you somehow." She handed him a bulky envelope. "It is dreadful to think of you sleeping in a tent out in the woods... even if it is temporary. This is a key for a room at the North Star. It's paid for... for as long as you need it... until you find a place of your own."

Jerry glanced at his father with an evil eye. "I don't need—"

"It's your mother's idea," Arthur interrupted. "Please… accept it as our penalty for not doing our job as good parents."

"It's a nice room," his mother smiled. "It's in the back and has a beautiful view of the valley."

Jerry walked them to their car and hugged them good-bye; it felt odd, but it didn't feel wrong. He watched them drive away, thinking about everything that had transpired during the last couple of days. He'd been on the edge of lost for so long, and then everything had suddenly changed all at once.

Munchkin hadn't been too impressed with the cement trucks growling in and out of Silver Spring for two days while Abbey's basement was taking shape. But now that the noisy trucks were gone, the cat slipped out onto the deck with Keith to view the early morning spectacle. A light fog hovered over the valley beyond the town. It was so peaceful; nothing was moving. Construction workers had not arrived yet, and it was much too early for anyone to be opening any of the shops except the bakery—there was someone there baking bread and pastries every morning by four o'clock.

Keith leaned against the deck railing, sipping his first cup of morning coffee, gazing out over the creation. Munchkin was on the railing, too, brushing against Keith's arm looking for some attention.

It saddened Keith to think that his partners courted the mining idea; it seemed so wrong to jeopardize the results of all their efforts. Silver Spring was their dream-come-true; Keith had never lost sight of that, but he feared that Robin and Grant had. Somehow, he had to convince them otherwise.

No one else on the construction crew was near Paul Marshall as he probed the earth with his shovel at the bottom of the trench along the side wall. He was sure he had left a pry bar there during the dismantling of the concrete forms. About midway the shovel blade struck something solid and metallic. Paul poked a few times at the object hidden beneath the soil that had been trampled over it, following along the length of the bar. He scraped away some of the dirt to expose one end. Reaching down he grasped the tool, but it did not move easily. The hooked end of the bar was apparently caught between some rocks. He dropped the shovel and gripped the bar with both hands, twisting, tugging, lifting. Whatever the hook was caught in seemed to be moving a little. With all his strength, Paul gave one last hard pull. The steel bar came free, but so did the rock that had held it captive. Paul stooped down to examine the rock more closely, as it seemed to have a strange color. But there was little time for him to get a better look; in the next instant, he felt the ground he stood on give way under his weight. With nothing to grab but dirt that simply crumbled in his clenching fist, he sensed that he was falling. It happened so quickly that he scarcely had time to let out a yell. And then it seemed as though he was sliding along a smooth rock surface, plummeting down a steep incline, his head striking several times against something very solid behind him. But it was so very dark; not a sliver of light anywhere. Surely he was falling into the depths of hell, and he was powerless to do anything about it.

Then, as quickly as the fall had begun, it ended abruptly as Paul lay sprawled awkwardly in a heap on what seemed to be a flat rock surface. He tried to move, but sharp pains shot through his right leg. The skin on his left shoulder burned, and his head throbbed. His hard hat had been knocked off in the fall. He felt around as far as he could reach with his good hand, but there was nothing but the dirt and stone rubble that had fallen with him. Darkness was so absolute, he could not determine into what kind of a place he had landed, but he could sense a great expanse. He could hear water trickling somewhere in the distance. He realized the chill of the air about him. And then there was nothing as he succumbed to unconsciousness.

Far above him, two other workmen had heard Paul's shout as he fell. They hurried to the trench where they last saw him, but they only found a shovel beside a hole in the ground, three feet long, two feet wide. They peered down into the hole and called out: "PAUL! PAUL! ARE YOU DOWN THERE?"

Their excited voices attracted others, and soon there were several more of the work crew gathered at the top of the trench looking down on the two who had discovered Paul's mishap. "What's going on down there? Is somebody hurt?"

Because it was still early in the day, there weren't a large number of shoppers and tourists yet to complicate the situation, but the frantic shouts of distress drew a few store clerks out of their shops. Clearly, there had been an accident, and the curious onlookers could only speculate the grim outcome.

Jerry had been raking smooth an area in the garden in preparation of planting some rose bushes, and at the same time enjoying a chat with his new-found friends, Clancy and his chum, Edward. He stopped the raking, cocked his head toward the ruckus at the construction site.

"Sounds like maybe someone got hurt over there," he said. "I'm gonna see if there's anything I can do to help."

He let the rake drop to the ground and started running toward the commotion, only to discover half-way there that his two companions were right at his side. When he arrived at the scene, he skirted around the crowd to get to a clear vantage point. One of the men continued to call down into the hole: "PAUL! CAN YOU HEAR ME? ARE YOU ALL

RIGHT? PAUL!" But there didn't seem to be any response.

Dave Parish had joined the two others next to the hole. "I called for an ambulance," he said. "But someone has to go down there to get him out." Just then another crewman threw a coil of heavy nylon rope down to him. Dave looked at the hole, and then to the other workers, all of whom were husky fellows, as was he, and would only add to the risk of negotiating through such a small passage. He had shined a high-powered lantern into the chasm, seeing nothing but a narrow opening between two walls of solid rock that an-gled away from his line of sight. "Who wants to give it a try?" he said desperately.

"I'm not going down that hole," one man said, and his sentiments were repeated among the others. It was obvi-ous that everyone was equally afraid of what they could not see.

"I'LL GO!" Dave heard a voice call out. He looked up to see Jerry Stevens waving to him, and before he could object, Jerry jumped down the embankment to the three men there. "Tie that rope around me... give me that lantern... lower me down there. I'm small enough to fit."

Jerry was, perhaps, the only person there who knew what to expect. The nameless boy had told him of the tun-nels and caverns under the town left behind by the Nine-teenth Century miners; he was about to find out if it was all true.

"I can't let you go down there," Dave Parish said. "It's gonna be dangerous."

"Less dangerous for me than for any of these other hulks," Jerry responded. "You've obviously got a seriously injured man down there! He needs help, and I'm quite capable of helping him."

Dave Parish eyed Jerry up and down. "Hey... you work for Keith, don't you?" He finally recognized the young man.

"Yes," said Jerry. "I'm the gardener... and I'm also the elf on the Crystal Palace stage who works magic." He was already tying a large loop in the end of the rope. When he slipped into the loop so that it would support him under his arms, he took the light from Parish. "Now start lowering me down there. When I tug on the rope, pull me back up." He stepped backwards into the hole, disregarding the threat to his own safety, and as the two other men held a firm grip on the rope preventing him from dropping too fast, Jerry disappeared into the darkness.

Noise from the spectators reduced to whispers and murmurs; Paul Marshall's name had circulated among the crowd, so everyone knew who was at the bottom of that hole—if there was a bottom. Jerry Stevens' name was heard, too, as well as concerns of the safety of this brave soul.

"What happened?" Keith asked Dave Parish. Word of the accident had been delivered to the Tanglewood offices, and Keith rushed to the site.

"I don't know for sure," Dave explained. "A couple of my men heard Paul yelling for help, but all they found was this hole, and no Paul. He must've fallen down there."

"What's at the end of that rope?" Keith asked.

"Your boy... that Stevens kid."

"What?"

"I think his name is Jerry."

"Why is he—"

"He volunteered... he *insisted* on going down there to help Paul... that is, if Paul can be helped."

"But Jerry? Why did you let him go down there?"

"He's the only one of us who could fit into that hole."

Another voice from up on the bank called down to them: "You mean, Dave, that he was the only one who had the guts to do it."

"Well, yes, that, too."

"We'd better get an ambulance on the way," Keith said.

"I've already called," Dave replied. "They should be here within ten minutes."

As Jerry was eased down through the passageway, he kept the light pointed downward, watchful of any hazards in his path. He thought it was a good thing he wasn't claustrophobic, as the space between the two walls was quite limited. And he wondered what he had gotten himself into.

After several minutes of creeping downward, his light beam found Paul Marshall lying motionless, and a few seconds later his feet touched down on the flat surface beside the injured man. The man's face was cut and bruised, and one leg was twisted to an abnormal position. Jerry put his ear to the man's chest. There was a heartbeat, and he seemed to be breathing. He patted the man's chest vigorously. "Paul! Paul! Can you hear me?"

When there was no response, Jerry said softly, "Okay, Paul… we gotta get you outa here, and it's probably a good thing you're out cold so you don't feel anything when they pull you up."

Jerry slipped the rope from his own torso and manipulated it around Paul in similar fashion, hoping the men at the other end wouldn't be too forceful. He propped Paul up against the incline so he was pointed in the right direction, and gave a gentle tug on the rope. The slack tightened, and Paul began his slow return to the surface. Jerry trained the light on him until he was out of sight.

For the first time, Jerry realized how cold it was; he wasn't dressed for it, and now that the adrenaline rush had subsided, his body was reacting to the forty degree difference in temperature; he shivered as if he were standing in a Chicago blizzard clad only in his underwear. He had to get moving... get the blood circulating. It would take time to get Paul to the surface. Jerry turned and pointed the lantern away from the passage. His eyes widened with amazement. He was standing at one side of a huge cavern, at least a hundred feet wide and twice as long, and the ceiling raised forty or fifty feet above him. The sound of water—like that of a gurgling stream—echoed placidly.

He started walking toward the other side of the cavern, nearly stumbling over the narrow gauge steel rails that had once carried the ore cars to an opening in the side of a hill. When he neared the far vertical wall, he saw what that old miner, Calvin Henshaw had seen so long ago. The lantern's beam reflected the soft, silvery glow from the rock, and piles of stones varying in size, apparently chiseled from the wall, lay strewn about the floor, the remaining ore left behind after the fatal cave-in that had closed the mine forever. Jerry stooped down and rummaged through the stones until he found a couple of small ones—about the size of a half-dollar—and put them in his pocket.

"It's Paul!" Dave Parish exclaimed as Paul became visible at the top of the passage. It was obvious that Paul was unconscious, but it was impossible to determine the extent of his injuries. Two EMTs applied a neck brace and then carefully lifted Paul from the hole and placed him on a gurney that could be hoisted up from the trench with ropes. A brief examination before they moved him more prompted them to apply an air splint to his right leg. An oxygen mask was fitted over his face, and then two more ambulance attendants began hoisting the gurney out of the trench, a growing crowd watching in concerned awe.

Dave Parish, Keith, and the other two crewmen had scrambled out of the trench and were at the back door of the ambulance van where the EMTs were attending to Paul.

"I'll go with him to the hospital," Dave said, and he climbed in. The doors closed and the ambulance drove away, lights flashing and siren screaming.

Keith turned to the two workmen. "Did you see what happened?" he asked.

Both shook their heads. "No," one said. "We heard Paul yell, but we were around the corner so we didn't see him fall. The ground must've collapsed over that hole, and he just fell in."

Keith thought about the warning that he, Robin, and Grant had heard from the unidentified boy via Jerry. JERRY! He was still at the bottom of that hole waiting for the rope to be dropped back down to him.

"Get that rope down to Jerry!" Keith said. "By now he's probably thinking we forgot about him."

Jerry continued his exploration, walking the entire length of the cavern, occasionally stopping to do a few jumping jacks to keep warm. Four more tunnels went off in different directions from the big room; he shined the light into each one, but he decided not to venture into them for safety's sake. The water he heard was trickling from the far wall into a pool and running off into one of the tunnels. He scooped up a cupped handful of the cold water and put it to his lips; it was fresh and clean, and it felt good on his tongue. The place was truly a marvel; no one but him had seen it in the past century or more; no one but him knew of the wealth contained in this abyss beneath Silver Spring, so close, yet so far out of reach.

Wondering how long he had been there in the cavern, he realized that he had lost track of the time. He sprinted back to the passage expecting to see the rope waiting for him, but there was no rope. Jerry pointed the lantern beam up into the dark passage, but there was nothing but rock.

"HEY!" he called out. "IS ANYBODY UP THERE?"

He heard no response.

"HEY! CAN ANYBODY HEAR ME?"

Still no answer.

"They must still be busy getting Paul out and into an ambulance," he said to himself. But it had been a long time, he thought. An ambulance crew would certainly work faster than that to get a seriously injured person on the way to a hospital. There had to be another reason the rope hadn't been let down to him. And then it occurred to him that he had traversed over several humps and angles along the inclined wall on his way down. The possibility existed that the rope was hung up on one of those humps; they would not know that up there at the top.

He studied the fissure in the rock strata; he thought if he could get up to where it narrowed to form the passage, he could put his back to one side and use his feet on the other to work his way up. It would be slow progress, but it would get him out of this dungeon. His rubber-soled shoes gripped the rock surface somewhat, but the angle of the incline was so steep, and the surface so smooth that he couldn't get a hand hold to help pull himself up. The narrow part of the passage was about four feet above him, just out of reach. After several tries always resulting in him sliding back down, he found the right spot; it seemed almost as if he had gotten a boost from behind, but he knew there was no one else there. With the strength in his arms pushing against each side of the opening, he managed to get up inside the narrow, his back against one wall and his feet braced against the other. But now the lantern was at the bottom, pointed up toward him, but way out of reach, and he wasn't going back down to get it.

Slowly he inched his way upward; the farther he went, the darker it became. He knew, however, from his downward journey, there was no chance of getting off course; on either side, the opening narrowed to only a few inches, making it impossible for a body to get through. His only real hazard was losing his grip; if his feet slipped, he could end up at the bottom again, and in a condition similar to Paul's when he found him.

Keith watched as the rope dropped down. They had fed as much rope—more—as had gone down with Jerry the first time. But there was no tug from the other end. Nothing. Then an unfamiliar voice from nearby said, "The rope's getting hung up... pull it back up and attach a weight on the end." Keith looked up to see a young man staring at him, a concerned expression on a face that *was* familiar to him; it was the fellow he had seen several times near the construction site. But this wasn't the time to start a conversation.

"He's right!" Keith yelled. "Pull up the rope!"

The rope was brought up again. Keith looked around for something to attach as a weight. The pry bar that Paul had found lay in the dirt next to the hole. He had dropped it when he fell. Keith picked up the bar and tied the end of the rope to it securely. "Okay… drop it back down."

They listened to the bar clinking against the rock wall as it pulled the rope down. The sound became less distinct until it faded away completely.

Jerry had progressed upward; how far he didn't know for sure. He paused for a breather, and while he rested he heard a metallic clunking sound that seemed to be coming from far above his head. And it was coming closer. Something was falling toward him. He wanted to get out of the way, but there was nowhere to go. He shielded the top of his head with his arms, hoping to deflect whatever the object was. As it passed, it struck his left leg a sharp blow, causing enough pain for Jerry to release the grip of his left foot. But his right foot was still planted firmly against the rock, barely holding him in position.

Then as the noisy clatter dropped below him, he heard the rope scuffing along the rock beside him. He felt with his hands in the dark and found the nylon rope just a foot to his left, still on its downward slide. Then the clanging stopped with one final thud and the rope stopped falling. The metal object had reached the floor.

Jerry gripped the rope tightly with both hands and gave a strong, quick jerk. The rope started hauling him upward, and he was thankful that he would soon see daylight again.

39

Jerry covered his eyes to block the bright sunlight as soon as his hands were free from the rope. Several people were clustered around him, but he only recognized one voice—Keith's. "Are you okay, Jerry?" Keith asked. "Are you hurt at all?"

"Just a bruise on my leg from whatever that was tied to the end of the rope. It got me on the way down."

"It was a pry bar," Keith said. "It was the only thing I could find in a hurry to weight the rope." He looked down at Jerry's leg and saw the blood. It was more than just a bruise.

"Did you get Paul outa there okay?" Jerry asked.

"Yeah, thanks to you. He's probably at the hospital by now."

Jerry's eyes started adjusting to the light; he noticed the number of people gathered around him. He stepped forward to get away from them, and then his left leg let him know that he had not come out of the hole unscathed. The slight limp was noticed.

"Let's get you to the hospital, too," Keith said. "I'll get my car."

"No," Jerry said. "I'll be fine."

"You're going," Keith insisted. "Your leg is bleeding."

A couple of the workmen helped Jerry up out of the trench while Keith went for his car. "What was down there?" they asked. "What did you see?"

"A big black hole," Jerry replied. "Didn't see much of anything… it was very dark." He didn't think he owed a detailed report to these guys. He was grateful to them for pulling him out, but that's as far as it went. Anything else was going to be strictly between him and Keith.

"Get something to cover that hole," Keith called out. He had returned with his Grand Prix. "I don't want anyone else falling." Then he put an arm around Jerry to help him to the car.

"Does it hurt bad?" Keith asked when they were well on the way.

"A little," Jerry replied.

"I'm really sorry about that pry bar. How did it happen to hit you?"

"I was already on my way up the passage. It had been quite a while since they pulled Paul out. I kinda figured the rope got hung up somewhere on the rocks."

"That's exactly what that kid said. So I found the pry bar and tied it on."

"What kid?" Jerry asked.

"Oh, yeah… that kid that you've been talking to… that I've seen hangin' around the construction site."

"Oh, you must mean Clancy. Was his friend, Edward with him?"

"No one else, that I saw. So, what was at the bottom of

that hole?" Keith said. "You took a lantern down with you, didn't you?"

"Yeah, Keith... I saw plenty, but I didn't tell the others when they asked because I wanted to tell you first."

"Good," Keith said. "I appreciate that."

"That passageway was just a big crack in the rock... just barely wide enough to get through in some places, and it went at an angle all the way down. It ended in a huge cavern... like the ones Clancy told me about."

Keith slowed the Grand Prix as he came into the outskirts of Wellington. "So do you think it was part of the old mine?"

"Oh, it was part of the mine, all right. The rails for the ore cars were still there."

"Could you see how big the cavern is?"

"It's big... at least a hundred feet across, and maybe two hundred feet long, and more tunnels going off in different directions."

"The passage went down at an angle?"

"Yeah... that cavern is probably right under the Crystal Palace and the Royal... right under Main Street."

Keith pulled the car into a parking space just across from the emergency entrance, turned off the motor, and just sat there staring at Jerry. "So... what else did you see?"

"Keith... there's silver down there. Lots of it. The walls and the ceiling of that cavern glowed silver in the lantern light." He dug one of the sample stones out of his pocket and handed it to Keith. "Clancy was right about that miner... what's his name... Henshaw?"

Keith took the stone from Jerry and examined it closely. "Jerry," he said. "You have to promise me that you won't breathe a word of this to anyone."

"I wasn't planning on it."

"What about Paul? Did he see it?"

"I doubt it," Jerry said. "He was out cold when I got to him."

"Okay," Keith said, thinking deeply about what to do next. "Let's get you into the emergency room... get that leg fixed up."

Jerry put his hand on Keith's shoulder, holding him from exiting the car. "Keith? Will you make me a promise?"

"Sure. If I can."

"Promise me that you won't do anything to harm Silver Spring. If you could just see the look in Clancy's eyes when he... well... he's really worried about what will happen. I don't know the whole reason, but Silver Spring is pretty special to him."

"Yeah, I know, Jerry. It's kinda special to all of us."

40

Keith couldn't lie to his partners. He wanted to, but he couldn't. "Jerry was in one of the mine shafts," he said at the next early morning meeting. "One of the caverns that was blocked off by the cave-in. The cave-in that we saw eight years ago."

"That's where he rescued Paul Marshall?" Robin said.

"Yes."

"So that passage led into the mine?" Grant asked.

"Yes. It's a fissure in the bedrock. It could never have been used as an entrance. Jerry said it went at a steep angle, and the direction puts the cavern he was in right under Main Street, the Crystal Palace, and the Royal building."

"Well, just how big is this cavern?"

"He estimated it to be at least two hundred feet across... maybe more. The ceiling is a good fifty to sixty feet above the floor."

"Is he sure he was in a mine shaft?"

"He found railroad tracks... like the ones we saw coming out of that cave-in. And he brought with him a little sample." Keith tossed the stone on the table. Robin and Grant stared at its silvery sheen.

"So that kid was right," Robin said.

"That kid..." Keith paused and took a deep breath. "Let me tell you about that kid. Jerry has been talking to him quite regularly; he told me about him while we were waiting at the hospital. His name is Clancy, and he seems quite concerned about what will happen to Silver Spring. He told Jerry that he's been watching over it for many years. He told Jerry that it would break his heart to see mining here again… it would destroy Silver Spring."

Robin smiled. Grant frowned.

Keith continued. "Discovering this fissure means there could be more like it, and it also supports that warning of cave-ins; if they are disturbed they could collapse… and yes… our quaint little town could be swallowed in one gulp. We turned this place that everyone feared and loathed into something the people love and admire. I don't think we should take it away from them."

"How bad was Jerry's injury?" Robin asked.

"Not too bad… they bandaged the cut, and the doc said it would be sore for a while… told him to take it easy for a couple of days."

"Is he still staying at the North Star?"

"Yeah… and Kevin is gonna stop in once in a while."

"Good," Robin said. "I think I'll pay him a visit, too."

Robin's motive for seeing Jerry was more than just checking on an injured friend, although he was truly concerned for Jerry's welfare, and he would make certain that Jerry was comfortable and had everything he needed, and more. But just as important, this was an opportunity to talk to Jerry alone—to obtain some first-hand personal comments that he might not give so freely to others.

He knocked on the door of room 210. When it opened, Jerry stood there, dressed only in a pale blue bath robe. "Oh, hi Robin," he said, a little surprised with the visit. "Come in. I didn't expect to see you… I thought it was probably Kevin."

Robin stepped inside as Jerry limped to a table and two chairs in front of the window looking out over the valley.

"How are you feeling?" Robin asked.

"A little sore, but I'll live." Jerry invited his guest to sit down at the table. "Am I in some sort of trouble?"

"No... not at all. One of the reasons I'm here is to personally commend you for rescuing Paul Marshall. That took a lot of courage." He set his briefcase on the floor and sat down opposite Jerry.

Jerry shrugged his shoulders. "I just did what I thought was right. Is he okay?"

"His leg is in a cast, and he suffered a mild concussion, but he's home and he'll be fine... in about three or four months when his broken leg heals. Dave Parish said he'd offer you a job if you're interested, while Paul recovers."

Jerry laughed. "I worked construction jobs before I came here. I didn't really care for it... too noisy. And unless you're here to fire me..."

"Absolutely not!" Robin said.

"Then, tell Mr. Parish that I appreciate his offer... but no thanks."

"I'll be sure to pass that on to him."

Jerry pointed to one corner of the room and a small refrigerator, two-burner stove top, and a short counter with a sink. "Would you care for a cold drink? I have some Cokes in the fridge."

"Oh, no, thanks," Robin replied. "Wow! You have quite a place here... kitchen and all. And look at that view. D'ya see that wide spot in the creek just around the bend?"

Jerry peered out the window. "Yeah, I see it."

"Keith, Grant, Kevin, and I used to go swimming there."

"Was that when you were hunting for the treasure?"

"Yes, and quite a few times *after* we found it, too. But that was before we went off to college... before we knew that all this would happen someday."

"So what was the turning point? How *did* all this get started?"

"I guess it was the magic of the place," Robin said. "All the time we spent here when there were only a bunch of stone foundations hidden in the grass and weeds... and of course, Tanglewood, we allowed our imaginations to visualize the old town that had been here a hundred years before and what it must've been like to live here. And the more we learned about the town from studying the old journals—that got us out here looking in the first place—I think each of us began to nurture a fondness of the place, and we even joked then about cleaning up the old hotel to use for our hideout... a getaway when we needed one. Even then we knew that no one would ever disturb anything we wanted to leave here, because everyone was afraid of the place... the legend kept everyone away, so we knew we had a built-in security system."

"And did you do that?" Jerry asked.

"For the rest of that summer we were out here a lot, just to make sure no one was going to try to muscle in on our find. We kept it a well-guarded secret for the next four years. And every summer, between college terms, we spent most of our time here. No one knew about it except our fathers—we trusted them—and even they didn't realize how big the find really was... nor did we, at first. It was during our third year of college that we formed our real estate business and started the proceedings to buy the land."

"But weren't you afraid of someone coming along and finding your treasure?"

"Jerry? If you could've seen the trouble we went through to find it... I mean... nobody in their right mind would even try. And certainly no one would ever just stumble onto it."

"No one in their right mind? Are you saying that you—"

"We were kids then, Jerry. We weren't afraid of much. We were full of curiosity and cavalier spirit, and we didn't give much thought about the dangers we were subjecting ourselves to, much less the problems we'd face if we actual-ly *found* the treasure."

"So it laid there in that mine shaft four more years while you went to college?"

Robin nodded.

"And how could you manage to turn that much silver and gold into cash without anyone getting suspicious?"

"My father is an investment banker in Wellington. He has connections with a lot of people. He made most of the arrangements for us... everything legitimate. The whole thing was done over a long period of time, not all at once. No one ever raised an eyebrow."

"And that journal I keep hearing mentioned... Kevin never gave much detail, but he told me you found the clues in that journal that led you to it."

"Yes, Kevin was right about that," Robin said. "It led us to the treasure, but there's a lot more to it. We were able to reconstruct the town, and Keith designed the storefronts from the descriptions in that journal. All the streets have the same names they did in 1899."

Jerry's eyes were wide and bright, fascinated by Robin's story.

"In fact," Robin continued. "That's the other reason I came to talk with you." He reached down to his briefcase, opened it, and pulled out an aged brown leather-bound book. He carefully laid it on the table.

Jerry's eyes opened wider. "Is that it?"

Robin saw the intrigue in Jerry's face. He smiled. "Yes, this is it. I don't usually let it leave my office, and most of the time it's locked in the safe. But I thought there was good reason to bring it with me today... for you to see." He laid his hand on the book, as if to protect it. "But you must promise me, Jerry, that what you're about to see is kept in strict confidence."

"You have my word."

Robin opened the cover to reveal the first page and turned the book for Jerry's reading perspective.

Jerry read aloud: *"My Journal, Clancy Crane."* For a moment, it didn't register to him, and then, suddenly his expression became that of total wonderment. That's... that's... the name of the fellow who..." His voice trailed off.

Robin finished the sentence for him: "Who told you about the mines." Then he flipped some pages of the journal to where he had placed a marker. "Read a little of this," he said to Jerry.

Jerry read: *"Joey and Eddy came by yesterday morning... They wanted to explore the Indian caves... Joey's black dog Bear and Eddy's yellow dog Duke were with them..."*

"The other day," Robin said, "You mentioned to Kevin that another boy and a dog were with the fellow you've been talking with."

"Yes," Jerry replied.

"Does that boy have a name?"

"Edward. And his dog's name is... Duke."

Jerry read the lines in the journal again and then stared curiously into Robin's eyes.

"I don't know how it's possible, either," Robin said. "I don't have an answer... if there *really is* an answer." He turned some more pages back to another marker and instructed Jerry to read the passage about Tom Hargrove, the newspaper man that had become quite good friends with Clancy Crane by 1895.

Jerry read the page.

Robin pulled a newspaper from his attaché. It was a copy of the Wellington Daily News containing the reviews of *Midsummer Night's Dream*. He pointed to the article, and the byline in particular.

Jerry read: *"By Tom Hargrove."*

"That's the reporter who Kevin met in the theater on your opening night..." Robin said. "A couple of days before this article was published."

"But how..."

Robin shrugged his shoulders. "I checked with the Daily News office last week. The only address they have for *this* Tom Hargrove—the one who filed your play review—is the address of our print shop... that is where the old Silver Spring newspaper office was."

Jerry paged through the journal, reading more of Clancy's entries here and there; when he came to the episode of Oliver Pratt getting killed during his arrest, he read thoroughly and completely, every word. "So the sheriff didn't know about all the silver and gold that he hid in the mine... just three bars. Nobody knew the rest of it was even missing!"

"That's right," Robin said. "There were rumors about a treasure at Silver Spring, but no one really knew what it was. Some speculated that it was Jeremiah Crane's fortune; that was only false assumptions. And some were convinced that it was stolen bank loot... which turned out to be true, but it was found in 1968, and it was only three thousand dollars."

"So... what are you gonna do about the mining now?" Jerry asked. "I'm sure by now Keith has told you about my experiences down in that hole."

"He did. We've been discussing the issue at length ever since you first told us about your conversation with Clancy. And now you've shed some new light on the subject. We're considering all the options."

"Robin," Jerry said. "If you could just see the sorrow in Clancy that I have seen when he talks about it... if you could feel the anguish in his voice. He loves this place, and he's so afraid that the mining will destroy it again. Quite frankly, Robin, I'm afraid of that, too."

"We are quite aware of the possible consequences, and we'll do what we have to do."

41

All of Silver Spring was humming with activity. The County Historical Society was getting ready to start guided tours of the smelter ruins—their first step in raising funds for the new museum;. Merchants were moving into the recently completed store buildings on Main Street. Tourists and locals blended together; some were there to shop; some were there for the theater; some were there to absorb the history; and some were there merely to enjoy the unique atmosphere.

For Jerry, the days seemed to run away like wild horses over the hills. Within three days he was walking with just a slight limp. In a week, the limp was gone entirely, and he was back to work.

He had plenty to think about. The visit from his family had started the college mill grinding again—something he had set aside for the past two years. During all that time, his mindset was keeping him from thinking he was ready to go back to school. Maybe he hadn't been ready. But now that his father would not demand his return to Northwestern, and was willing to release the finances to another college of Jerry's choice, getting back to the books didn't seem so out of the question anymore. Kevin was getting some contacts lined up for him at the university, and he could soon start the registration process.

But there were other things on his mind, as well. Jerry had become the link between the owners of Silver Spring and a mysterious faction of people that no one could positively identify other than a strange coincidence of names. It seemed that only one of them—Clancy—would communicate with no one else but Jerry. His warnings of possible disaster had caused quite a stir.

The construction site accident had opened Pandora's Box. Jerry couldn't help but think that he had made a grave mistake by telling Keith the truth about what he had seen in the mine tunnel. He probably should have just kept quiet about the silver down there; he wouldn't have stimulated the new interest in mining at Silver Spring. But it was too late to think about changing his story now. What was done was done.

Clancy and Edward would come by the park for a visit with Jerry at times when Kevin wasn't there helping. They talked about everything, and sometimes they went with Jerry on the utility tractor and trailer to the creek to find some good landscaping rocks. "Onward," Edward would say, pointing toward the valley. "Onward to the great waters where we shall ferret out the mighty gems for the king's garden."

Every time their conversations ended with the same question from Clancy: "Any news about the mining?"

Every time Jerry told him that no decisions had come forth.

After watching Abbey's Restaurant construction for over two weeks, Keith could almost smell the aroma of Ranch Burgers and Curly Fries. Although it was now a recognizable building, it would still be two or three weeks yet until he could sink his teeth into one of Abbey's specialty burgers. In the meantime, he had plenty of work to do for clients, and planning the future for Silver Spring. He and his partners had been at odds over the question of reopening the mine under the streets; they had made a decision, and they had invited Kevin and Jerry to join them at their early morning meeting in the saloon and had given them the news. They deserved to be the first to know.

On his days off—Saturday and Sunday—Jerry usually hiked into Wellington, deposited his paycheck at the bank, got some cash, and then shopped for his personal necessities while his clothes washed and dried at the Laundromat. He'd treat himself to a burger and fries at Abbey's downtown, and then with backpack filled with clean laundry, he hiked back to his campsite in the wilderness.

Saturday routines had recently changed, though, now that he had taken up residency at the North Star with its own laundry room. And Kevin had given him access to the maintenance pickup truck for occasional trips into town, even if it was just for personal reasons. His lifestyle was changing from that of a nomad, to at least a level of mediocrity, and he was sure that it would be changing a lot more.

As Jerry wandered the Silver Spring streets on this very busy tourist weekend, he searched the sea of ever-changing faces in hopes to find Clancy. At the site of the new *old* barn, the hammers and saws were silent now as the construction workers enjoyed a day off, too. He thought they had outdone themselves on this one—the old weathered boards on the outside walls facing the Square gave the appearance that the "Livery Stable" had been there for a hundred years; it was certainly a wonderful addition to Silver Spring.

He passed by his beloved Market Square garden that was receiving its usual share of attention from a throng of admirers. Jerry was thankful that he had been given the opportunity to create such a centerpiece for this magnificent place.

On his casual walk by the Royal building, Jerry couldn't resist the tantalizing, delicious smells coming from the bakery; he went inside. The day just didn't seem complete without a warm cinnamon roll fresh out of the oven.

Across the street the Crystal Palace was gearing up for the weekend shows, a Dixieland jazz band. Jerry had seen their bus in the hotel parking lot that morning, and now the roadies were unloading their equipment truck at the theater side doors next to the stage. Watching them brought back joyous memories of his nights on that stage; he wondered if it would ever happen again.

Next door, the sounds of power tools made another kind of music as carpenters and electricians readied Abbey's Restaurant for its opening. Like Keith and Kevin, Jerry, too, was now looking forward to the best burgers on the planet, right there in Silver Spring.

Just down the street at the Wild West Bank building—that wasn't actually a bank, but merely housed an ATM for the convenience of Silver Spring patrons—Jerry paused a while to watch the Wellington Players perform the usual Saturday mock bank hold-up. He'd never seen it. They had attracted a generous crowd, obviously entertained by "One-eyed Bart" and his band of black hat and duster clad bank robbers. As the spectators watched from the street, Bart and his gang entered the small structure; a few gunshots were heard from inside; moments later they nervously stumbled out again carrying stuffed canvas bags. Their escape, however, was cut short when the sheriff and his posse arrived. Jerry recognized the sheriff and one posse member played by Adam Hall and Derek Collins; he had shared a backstage dressing room with them during the run of *Midsummer Night's Dream.*

Any Wild West bank robbery couldn't be complete without a six-gun shootout; these players staged a good one, culminating in the capture of One-eyed Bart and the recovery of the loot. It was a great little show, and the crowd loved it.

Jerry thought he had been quite observant during his wandering that day, but nowhere had he seen Clancy. He wondered if his friend had become discouraged and had left Silver Spring to avoid the heartaches the future might bring. Then it occurred to Jerry that Clancy had always *found him*, usually where he was working in his garden projects, and not just some random spot on the street with other people around.

It made perfect sense; Jerry was the only person—as far as he knew—with whom Clancy had ever communicated. He seemed shy and reluctant to interact with others. He invented reasons to leave abruptly whenever Kevin came near. Keith had seen him, but had never talked with him. And Robin had made it perfectly clear that Clancy still remained a mystery to him.

Yes. It made perfect sense to Jerry now. He headed to the park. There he would be alone, and if Clancy was still around, he would come.

Surveying the park area, Jerry saw several weeks' work ahead of him to complete the project. But what a wonderful spot to spend the rest of the summer. Gentle breezes blew up from the valley; eagles soared overhead; the smell of pine and wildflowers filled the air. It was no mystery why Robin, Grant, Keith, and Kevin had been so attracted to this place; it had been something more than the treasure.

To them, unlike most people, the realism of a prior century hadn't seemed so far-fetched, like merely a shadow cast by a dream.

Jerry sat on one of the new park benches, the afternoon sun warming the breeze. Occasional hikers passed by, and soon Jerry realized they were probably the reason Clancy didn't show up. He moved to the shade of a small birch grove beyond the restrictive hedge along the cliff, out of sight to passersby. Settling down on the cool grass with his back to a tree, he had a perfect view of the valley vista.

He thought about his family, his brother in particular, who was still just a vague blur to his memory, but at least it was a blur, which was more than it had been for the past two years.

He thought about going back to school, contemplating what life would be like in a different scholastic environment.

He thought about travel, wondering if he would ever venture out again. His friends and his love of for this place kept him here now, but he knew he was destined to see the world... *after* he finished college.

And then his eyes captured the scuffed brown shoes, the faded denim trousers held up by leather suspenders over shoulders draped with the faded blue cotton shirt, the chestnut brown hair that fluttered in the breeze and the cosmic blue eyes that flashed a friendly *hello*.

Clancy sat down in the grass beside Jerry. "I've been waiting for you," he said.

"I was looking for you all over Silver Spring," Jerry replied. "But then I thought you might find me here."

"Too many people in town today," Clancy said.

They sat there for a while gazing out over the peaceful

valley without saying anything, and then Jerry broke the silence. "They've made a decision about the mine."

Clancy cocked his head and stared into Jerry's eyes.

"Kevin and I were invited to their morning meeting... we were the first to hear."

Clancy didn't say anything. He just listened.

"Robin said they were sure there's a fortune in silver under the streets. It would put a lot of people to work getting it out, and it would bring wealth to many."

"So... they'll reopen the mine?" Clancy said sadly.

"No. It would be unfair to all the business people who have invested their time and money and effort in Silver Spring's revival to turn it into a dusty, noisy place that no one would want to visit. And it wouldn't be fair to take it away from you."

Clancy's stare returned to the creek in the valley. "So... Silver Spring will stay like it is?"

"Yes, Clancy. Silver Spring will stay like it is."

"So..." Clancy said as he gazed all around with a broad smile. "This must be heaven."

"Close..." Jerry replied. "It's Montana."

ABOUT THE AUTHOR

Born into a farm family in the late 1940s, J.L. Fredrick lived his youth in rural Western Wisconsin, a modest but comfortable life not far from the Mississippi River. His father was a farmer, and his mother, an elementary school teacher. He attended a one-room country school for his first seven years of education.

Wisconsin has been home all his life, with exception of a few years in Minnesota and Florida. After college in La Crosse, Wisconsin and a stint with Uncle Sam during the Viet Nam era, the next few years were unsettled as he explored and experimented with life's options. He entered into the transportation industry in 1975 where he remained until retirement in 2012

Since 2001 he has thirteen published novels to his credit, and one non-fiction history volume, *Rivers, Roads, & Rails.* He was a featured author during Grand Excursion 2004.

J.L. Fredrick currently resides at Poynette, Wisconsin.